INTEGRITY HAS NO BOUNDS

LUCIFER'S BREED MC
BOOK 2

BY RYDER DANE

This Work is fiction. All organizations, events, and characters named or referenced in this work are products of the author's imagination or used fictitiously.

ISBN-10# 1-945012-08-0

ISBN-13# 978-1-945012-08-2

Cover Model James Xavier
Photographer Holly Fain

Edited by Vinvatar Publishing

Artwork by Jess Buffett Graphic Designs

Published by Vinvatar Publishing
Website: Vinvatar.com

TABLE OF CONTENTS

PROLOGUE

Curtis Mack was beginning to feel his age. He'd been a saddle tramp most of his adult life, and his ass and spine felt every one of those twenty years. His journey through life had begun in the hills of the Great Smokey Mountains, and now he found himself back in the area of his childhood. He wasn't here to visit family, they were gone from this earth now, and he felt no attachment to the place.

He was trailing some fuckers who were double dealing the club. With his position as a Nomad of Thor's Legion MC, one of his duties was to protect the club from Rogues and members who could potentially bring the heat down on their heads.

The information he was working off was iffy at best, but his informant certainly knew the area, and the people around the small Arkansas town. With the information he'd already had accumulated, along with his informant's information, it made sense. It also was the reason he was heading to Juanita, Missouri.

A while back, the area was plagued by a South American who wanted in on the territory to sell their drugs. Most of the small clubs had banded with the big boys and driven them out. One small club only paid lip service to the coalition of MCs and now that he knew the connection, it finally made sense. All he needed was to prove it, and that was the reason he was on the road tonight.

The other information he'd learned was of a more personal nature, and well, if it proved to be true, he would cross that bridge after dealing with the club's business first.

It wasn't until he saw the young man who owned the place that things cleared up. He knew this one, and for his old friend's sake, he would deal with this as soon as the man closed up for the night.

He waited for the last vehicle in the parking lot to leave, and went to the backdoor of the bar. The door hadn't been locked yet, but the fist that caught his jaw as he entered the building almost knocked him off his feet. He stood back and wiped the blood from his lip before grinning and returning a fist toward his assailant.

By the time he pulled his tired ass up from the floor, he was laughing.

"Goddamned, kid, you have a fuckin' jaw like your ol' man's, I think I broke a finger. It's good to see you again."

*****

Standing there, the shortest man, who both of the others deferred to, nodded for his minions to knock the boards back in place. He sat at the bar drinking a whiskey neat. It was the top shelf stuff, not the rotgut bar whiskey. The bartender poured him another and popped the tops from two icy cold cans of beer. He handed one to his peer and nodded to the boss man.

"I hate to bring this up, but the kid is getting snoopy. He asked me why I hadn't swept around the stage last week, and yesterday he stayed until after I usually close the place. I had to stuff a brick of the high grade into my fuckin' jacket and take it home with me last night."

The tallest of the three men sneered, "Maybe it's time to take him out. Sooner or later he'll contact his fuckin' father, and it will cause us so much trouble that it might disrupt our little enterprise here. You can always buy the place and run it, and no one will be the wiser. If we work it right, there won't be anything to stop us from going bigger, maybe expand our territory." He looked toward the man who was staring at the glass in his hand. "What do you think?"

Their leader took his time before answering, as if there might be another way to deal with the son of a very dangerous man. A man who could potentially bring this easy money to a humiliating halt. He looked at the two rough bastards that seemed to have personal interests invested in the death of the young man. He finished his drink and handed the glass to the bartender, "Do it, the roads around here are treacherous, accidents happen."

He hated having to hop down from the barstool, once on his feet, both men towered over his own five feet eight inch frame. They were dangerous men in their own right, but they would never reach the contacts he had and they needed him. It's what gave him the confidence to be alone in a room with them. As long as he made the deals and used his knowledge to pass their product, they would fall into line.

Finished with their business, the three men headed through the backdoor with no regards for anyone or anything because plans had been set and everything was falling into place. To them no one was smarter—a shame they didn't notice the small blinking light in the corner.

The backdoor slammed shut and the light went out before he moved silently in the tiny room. Another plan formed, it would devastate a few, but the outcome would be worth a little pain. Payback's a bitch.

CHAPTER ONE

John walked into the bar the club held the note on, looking for the owner. He spied her mounting the steps of the small dais and found himself a seat at the bar ordering a beer. He could wait, it wasn't like he had somewhere to be tonight. He planned to go home after this last stop.

The tables were full of people, some of them wore their desperation to find a significant other or just tonight's bed partner. The bartender handed him a draft beer he had yet to order, and told him the lady at table fourteen sent it. He nodded toward the table and saw Ronnie Davis with three other women. Ronnie didn't smile at him, she stared at him with what he could only describe as heat. He shook his head and told the bartender to take the drink to her. It surprised the man, but he shrugged and took the glass over to the woman. Ronnie smirked, put the glass to her lips and drank half of the contents without taking a breath.

He understood what she was doing, the challenge was what she thrived on, and she had him firmly in her sights. John didn't fuck around playing games when he wanted someone. He paid for his pleasures one way or the other, sometimes he'd take a chunk off the price of an oil change, or some repair that was too pricey for the vehicles owner to pay cash for. Sometimes it was money, or even dinner and a few drinks. He never took without giving back. Too many fuckers took advantage of women and vulnerable ones at that. No meant no as far as he was concerned, there were plenty of others who always said yes.

Ronnie was a beautiful woman, there was nothing innocent or complicated about her, and he wished they could be friends instead of him being her prey. He didn't like aggressive women, and she wore her independence like a neon light. If she were a man, she'd be the perfect companion, always ready for a new adventure, always ready to fight, just uncomplicated and fun to have around.

He rapped on the bar and ordered a longneck. The bartender gave him a shake of his head, but brought the bottle. He twisted his own cap and flipped the thing on the wooden surface before turning around on the stool to watch Stevie Hill begin to play her guitar. She played two acoustic pieces he didn't recognize, but still liked the music, and then she began singing. Her voice wasn't angelic as some women could be described as having. There was a rasp and he could only describe it as a halting earthy sound, he liked it. Her voice made him think of hot sex on cool sheets.

She fascinated him. Her hair was straw colored blond, and if he had to guess the length, it would be long. The way she twisted it in a knot at the back of her head made it difficult to tell. The first time he looked into her blue eyes, he felt his stomach tighten, and each time he watched her curvy body walk into a room, onto the stage, hell, she could be sitting twiddling her thumbs and his dick would wake up. She was probably five ten in height, and she had a smart mouth on her, but it didn't stop him from wanting her.

She was intelligent, and could really keep him on his toes to hold a conversation with her. It was damn difficult to multitask when she laughed. There was no restraint when she laughed, he'd been like a damn dog every time he caught sight of her, and if he were on his deathbed, the sound of her laughter would wake him up. Something he would do to just to see that smile.

He stayed away from this place as much as he could because of the woman on the stage. She took the place over when her brother left, and she was actually doing better at managing the business than her brother had been. She never made excuses, and was never late on a payment. It was why he was here tonight. Burger asked him to pick up the money for him, and since John couldn't come up with a legitimate reason not to come tonight, here he was, torturing himself with listening to the woman whose voice haunted his nights. The more he knew about her—the harder it was to keep himself from begging her for any little scrap of attention she might give him.

The reason he hadn't made any advances toward the pretty woman was she had no need of him. He knew it was fucked up thinking, but he liked things straight forward in every aspect of his life. Everything and everyone had a place or a niche in life, hers would be labeled as a possible lover. But where did he fit in her life? The second, and probably the most important reason was her brother. Viking had warned his MC brothers away from his little sister. A real man didn't cross the line when dealing with family, and John understood the man's reasoning, even if he didn't like it.

She was talented, and smart. She didn't need her vehicles worked on that she couldn't pay for. She didn't need him for protection, she had the entire MC chapter of Lucifer's Breed to take care of that. No one would fuck with her that had any sense. Her brother was a full patched member when he left her, and now that she was alone in the world, the brothers kept a close eye on her safety.

"Walk away, or kiss me" was the final words of the last song she sang, and she stared at John Handy as she voiced them. The big mechanic was far too tempting for her peace of mind. Every time she saw him, she wanted to ask him why he never asked her out. She could see and sense his interest in her, but he always collected the mortgage payment and left without allowing her to introduce any small talk between them. They had exchanged complete sentences maybe four times that she could remember, and it gave her hope each time they spoke. Yet he kept his distance, and she had no idea how to make him understand that she wanted him. She laughed at his jokes, tried her best to flirt with him without being too whorish, hell, the only thing she hadn't done was to install a stripper pole and invite him for a private show. The thought of his face if she did that made her smile.

She'd sung the last song, one she had written, just for him. It was doubtful he understood what it meant, but she could always hope. She set her guitar on the stand behind the stool she had perched on while she sang, and made her way toward the office where the safe was located. She needed to give him some information to take back to the club's president too, so when she got to the end of the bar, she tilted her head toward the door and looked at him.

He stood and set the empty on the bar, and she shifted her gaze to Leon, the bartender, who got her meaning and handed John another bottle as he made his way to where she stood.

He opened the door for her to pass through ahead of him, and she liked that—he had manners. She unlocked the office door with the key hanging on her wrist. He shut the two of them in the small room and stood by the door with his arms crossed and the unopened beer still held in his hand.

She went to the safe and placed her hand on the screen under the panel, which appeared to be a combination lock. It was a nice trick, and John nodded approvingly while he watched her.

"I needed to talk to one of you guys any way. I know that you don't want to be bothered, but could you sit down for a few minutes while I show you something?" She pulled the envelope from the stack of bills, and shut the safe, before turning to walk to her messy desk.

She sat down and watched as he sat in the chair in front of her. She handed the envelope to John and waited to see his reaction. He looked puzzled for a second, until he read the note she'd put in the envelope with this month's mortgage payment.

It was essentially an extortion note. Complimenting her on owning such a "popular, and well run establishment" and "we want to continue to see the place thrive, so for the meager price of one thousand dollars a month, cash only," they would provide security for both her, and the bar.

She could see the anger building in the big man.

His head came up, and his eyes pinned hers as he asked, "When did you get this, and why didn't you call the club?"

"I found the note last week. It was in a stack of invoices I was paying, and it kind of jumped out at me. No one seemed to know how it got on my desk, and no one remembers any strangers walking back into the hallway, so I figure it was probably one of the staff that dropped it in here. I didn't take it seriously enough before, because I didn't believe someone would be so stupid as to threaten a business the Breed had their tentacles into." She looked away to hide the pain she was felling from him. "My cat was a grouchy old Tom with a bad attitude toward strangers, and a habit of attacking men with bad intentions."

She stood, and came around the desk to stand in front of him, before saying, "This isn't a peep show so don't fear for your virtue, big boy." The long sleeved sweater she wore was pulled off her head, leaving her standing before him in a peachy-colored tank top with bruises on her upper arms, and around her throat.

The purple dots across the top of her breasts enraged him. One bruise would earn the fucker a beat down. This earned him death. There was a small cut on her neck where it was obvious to the man seeing it, was caused by a knife or another sharp object.

"I had a visitor night before last, he was in my place when I got home, sitting in the dark. He was on me before I could turn the lights on, or even scream. He said that bad things happen to good people, and that I should take the offer of protection seriously or he'd be back." She pulled the sweater back over her head and settled the cowl neck to hide the low lying bruising from prying eyes. "He killed my cat, and cut the mattress on my bed. I called the cops, and they have the report, and a sample of the man's blood and DNA. Tom must have scratched him, and he tried to wash the blood off in the kitchen sink."

She turned away and went back to her desk chair, still feeling shaken, but determined to remain as matter of fact as possible. There was no way she was going to break in front of this man. If it had been any of the other brothers of the Breed, she knew she'd probably be blubbering like a baby right now. John Handy had a habit of making her want to gain his respect, and crying like a five-year-old was not going to cut it around him. The one thing she needed from him was comfort, but it was the one thing she was sure he'd consider a glaring weakness.

"I need a gun. I have a puppy coming, but he won't be ready to leave his momma for at least another two weeks, and he won't be much help until he gets older anyway. I heard a motorcycle start up and leave when the man left, so I'm pretty sure it's an MC making the threats. Since it's not the Breed, I figure it's either the Burning Bastards or the Swamp Kings. They want the money in an envelope, and told me they'd be by to pick it up on the first of the month."

John hadn't expected this. Maybe problems with a patron, or a brother, but extortion? The bruises made him want to find the fucker who hurt her, and put the cocksucker in a casket. He'd damn sure never touch her again.

"Did he rape you?" He forced the words out through gritted teeth, because he wanted to do damage to someone or something right this minute, and he didn't want to give her the impression he might hurt her.

She kept her head down, pretending to look at the papers in her fingers that showed the way she was trembling from the way the corner edge appeared to be vibrating.

"I asked you a question." He stood and she jerked her head around to watch him, he could see she was spooked and he had his answer without her having to voice the words. She looked ashamed, and there was no way he would let her believe there was any reason for that.

He kept his steps short but continued toward her, cursing a blue streak very low under his breath, but she heard him and cringed inside. No matter how many times she'd told herself it hadn't been her fault, that she was not trying to entice the bastard, it didn't help. She looked at herself as less than she was three days ago, and the knowledge hurt her independent nature. She had to snap out of this feeling, like she had given herself to the pig. He'd laid that knife on her neck and pressed the blade into her flesh, which stopped her from fighting him.

John reached down and pulled her to her feet as she cringed backwards. He refused to stop pulling her to his chest, and she stomped on his booted foot, but it did no good. She opened her mouth to scream at him to leave her alone, but his lips were already sealing themselves with hers, and it confused her. His arms wrapped her body tightly to his and she stopped trying to push him away. She couldn't decide if it was the feeling of security she had while he held her to him, or the way her mind seemed to accept him as if he belonged in her arms like this.

How could she feel this way, especially after that animal had held her on the floor and took her body as if he owned it. The only pain she'd felt at the time was where his filthy fingers and hands held her down. His dick was not the weapon he must have delusions about. To her it was a loss of choice, and she almost hadn't called the cops. If her assailant hadn't promised her a repeat visit, she might not have told anyone.

"I will find the fucker who hurt you and you won't need to worry about him again. You are beautiful, smart, and talented, don't let him take any of that from you, Stevie." John kept his hold on her and rubbed his hands up and down her back. He dropped his forehead onto hers, "I promise, if it's the last thing I do, I'll make sure you're protected from him and his Swamp Rats. I plan to ask Baron, but I don't think it's the Bastards, the men I've met are assholes, but they seem like decent assholes. The Swamp Rats, now those fuckers are not above

16

any crime or dumb scheme. Extortion is one of their main incomes, too bad they decided to enter Breed turf."

He loosened his hold on her and leaned down for a quick kiss. "Yeah, I know I act like a caveman, you seem to bring out that quality in me, and truthfully, I like it." He set her back in her seat and went back to his own. "Now I need you to tell me exactly what happened, start to finish."

"John, I've already told the police everything that happened, I went to the hospital and they did a rape kit, and took pictures. I already told you everything that happened, so what exactly do you want to know? Will it make a difference in what happened for you to know I quit fighting the bastard when he put a knife to my neck? Believe me, I felt the same things any woman would when her choices consist of dying or giving in. I never saw his face, I felt his breath on my neck, and was creeped out when his whiskers dragged on my skin while he threatened to keep coming back because he liked me." She stared at him for a few minutes, then turned her head toward the plant in the corner.

"I was as frightened as I ever want to be in my lifetime, and he knew it, he liked it, and told me so. After he was finished, I laid on the floor for a long time, hating my weakness. I should have fought harder, I should have let him slice my neck up, I should have been more careful." She shook her head, not paying attention to the tears sliding down her cheeks. "He told me not to think his fucking me would let me off the hook on the payments. The next time he had to come and talk to me, he would be bringing a few other men with him." She drew a deep breath, let it out, and took another one for good measure to calm herself.

"I tried to tell him that he was making a big mistake, that I had a mortgage to pay to Lucifer's Breed, but he kept slapping me every time I tried to speak. Will it add to the story when you tell your friends about what happened, to know the inside of my cheeks are like hamburger from my teeth when he hit me? Will your club brothers laugh when they hear I can't go back to my home because I'm too afraid to?" She laughed bitterly, and turned back to look him in the eye.

"Will they think I'm a coward for giving into him, for sitting on the floor of my shower scrubbing my skin until it hurt to touch it? How about the hour I sat at the drugstore waiting for them to give me a morning after pill to make sure I wasn't carrying my rapist's kid. They might get a chuckle out of the fact I had to have blood drawn to check for STDs. It's routine now, did you know that?"

Her sinuses were so full of snot she had to grab a tissue and blow her nose noisily. She looked up at John, who'd sat through her pity party, and wondered what he was going to do now. "Look, I know I am coming off as a weak-kneed bitch, but that's how I feel. I know you're a good guy, but right now, men are not my favorite people. I'm just a little bit bitter."

John heard every word she spoke, and he understood her questioning his discretion, but she needed to learn he wasn't her enemy. "Stevie, look at me, I'm going to tell you this one time, and one time only. The next time you question my integrity, I will put your ass over my knee and spank it. I'm not getting off on hearing that some fucker had his dick in a woman I've been interested in for myself for a long fucking time now. The fact he hurt you and made you cry sealed his fate.

"As far as me telling the brothers' every detail, that won't happen, they will know what he did, but not a blow by blow, it's not necessary, and I wouldn't share anything that intimate with another person. I needed to hear what happened, because I want you whole when I sink my cock inside you, trust me, you will feel me when it happens, but I won't bruise you or take what you aren't willing to give me."

Stevie shook her head, *did he just say*, "What do you mean, your cock will be... Look, you don't have to take responsibility for me. I told you I'm going to buy a gun and the puppy will bark if anyone is around, he won't be much of a guard dog for a while, but I will have enough notice to be prepared in case it happens again. You don't have to play at being my lover, I'll be fine.

"I only told you because I know there would be hell to pay if Lucifer's Breed found out I was paying another MC for protection, and if something were to happen to the building or the business, I'll probably be in a shallow grave somewhere or they'll find my body in the middle of the bar cremated already. You all need to know who to blame if something happens, that's all I wanted the Breed to know."

John stood and placed the chair squarely in front of the desk. "You close the bar at midnight?" She nodded and he told her to stay inside of the building until he got back. "If you leave before I get back, you won't be happy to find yourself over my knee and cuffed to my bed until we get this sorted out."

"You can't tell me what to do, and you can stop threatening to spank me too, I'm a grown woman, and don't need a daddy."

The last few words were spoken to the room. John had left, rather than stick around to listen to her arguments it seemed.

She blew out a breath and scowled at the idea he seemed to believe her misfortune gave him permission to boss her around.

CHAPTER TWO

Baron stared at the normally stoic ex-Ranger, now arguably the best mechanic in this corner of the state. John Handy was also one of the few men Baron was damn glad to name as a friend. There might have been a handful of times in the past few years that he'd seen the man so animated. However, this time, Baron sensed it was something John considered personal.

It was about damned time as far as Baron could see. John had lit up every time Stevie Hill's name was mentioned. When Skids and Tank had speculated if she might be interested in a good time, John had threatened to castrate Skids if he went near the girl. Tank had raised his hands in the air in surrender that day. Neither man wanted to test John physically, but his reaction to their teasing had given them more than enough fodder to tease the big man later on.

"You know I have to try to settle this first, right? I'll call Pappy D and warn him off. But we know they won't listen until someone gets his ass beat. They will back off and come sneaking in again in a few months. That persistence is about the only good quality those fuckers can lay claim to." Baron took a list of numbers from the top drawer of the desk and scanned for the number of the Swamp Kings' clubhouse.

John had already shown the letter that Stevie had given him to Baron and Leech. Before Baron started punching in buttons, John spoke up. His words of intent to do damage to the man he wanted to see face to face puzzled Baron until he heard what the real reason for John's anger was about.

"You can tell that Swamp Rat that I want his fuckin' rat-faced bastard who threatened Stevie, I will find him, or they can give the bastard up. If I have to pick them cocksuckers off one at a time until I get the right one, then it's no skin off my back. I need the target practice."

Leech had been sitting in a chair with the legs propped up, and let the legs hit the floor. "John, clubs threaten people all of the time, hell, we have had to make threats to get our point across too many times to remember. We usually settle for busting a few heads until the next time they slither from the stinking vegetation."

John turned on Leech, and advanced toward him slowly with his hands fisted at his side. "Really? Tell me how many times have we tried to extort money from a woman, and sent someone to threaten her in a hands on way?" He grabbed the smaller man and raised him up to speak to him. "Do we send in fuckers to rape them and kill her fuckin' pet? Is that what we do? Do we leave hand sized bruises on her body, Leech? If that's what we do you can have this fuckin' patch and I'm outta here."

He released Leech after setting him back on his feet, and turned to Baron. "You are the Prez, I got mad respect for you and the brothers, but the fucker who raped and beat Stevie is mine, I find him, and God is the only one that will save the motherfucker from the reaper. You can tell that pussy cocksucker that for me. Anyone looking to stop me will have to stand in a fuckin' line, I'm going hunting, any of those Rats get in my way? Collateral damage."

He turned to leave the room and was knocked in the jaw with enough force to rock him on his feet. Leech came at him and John held up his hand to stop him from stepping closer. "You got one free, I'm too fuckin' pissed to keep my temper in check, and you pushed the wrong damned buttons. Hit me again and I'll hurt you, it's even as far as I'm concerned."

"What the fuck is wrong with you? I like Stevie too, but I wasn't told to begin with that she was hurt, you didn't say a damned word about it. Next time you lay hands on me it's on, buddy, I don't take that shit from no one, not you, not anybody. You know damned well we don't hurt women like that."

John nodded, and left the room.

Baron grinned at his friend. "You hit like a girl, that little bitch slap was like a love tap to a brother like John, I was afraid I was going to have to step in between him and your broken ass."

Leech shook out the hand he'd used to punch the man. "That fucker's jaw is like a damned rock." He sat down, still flexing his fingers, "He's got it bad for little Stevie. She must be special to him, I've never seen him so deadly intent on getting his hands on someone. If it was anybody but one of the Swamp Kings, I might say give them a heads up that he's a lethal fucker, but I think I'll let them find out for themselves."

Baron nodded, "Yeah, about that. They won't give up the son-of-a-bitch. I'll warn Ol' Pappy D, but that is all he gets, they know where the lines are drawn on the southern boundary. My money says they knew it was Breed territory, but thought they could intimidate a lone girl. They couldn't know it is part of our empire. I'm about to explain it to them in small words so they understand what I'm saying." He punched in the numbers to connect. "This is going to be interesting."

By the time he finished talking to Pappy D, he was shaking his head and wanting the drugged up fucker to run across his path soon. He looked at Leech.

"Well you heard what he said. The reason I put him on speaker is because you all think I'm shitting you when I say talking to him is like talking to one of the gators in that swamp those boys play in. Brains about the same size too. We might have to deal in a harsher way with them this time, they have ambitions."

Leech nodded. "Yeah, 'Causin' we be in ta ways of the Swamp Kings progress." He mimicked the voice of Pappy D. "I swear, man, it was all I could do not to laugh out while that mumble-mouth tried to speak English. Damn shame he's hiding in that stinking swamp if you ask me."

The two men shared a laugh, and Baron left for home. Gunner and Stretch were already there. And he was looking forward to sitting in his recliner after dinner and pulling her little ass down onto his lap. The thought stayed with him as he backed his bike out of the parking spot in front of the club.

Leech went into the bar and Myrtle set up his favorite beer when she saw him headed her way. He took the barstool next to Burger and gave him the rundown on their nemesis, the Swamp Kings.

Tank, Skids, and Joker were hanging out looking bored, so Leech and Burger walked over to a large table so the others could be in on the conversation. The Swamp Kings, better known as the Swamp Rats, were hated by the brothers in Lucifer's Breed.

Tank didn't have a lot to say, the man was almost as quiet as John normally was, but Skids made up for any slack in the vocal denouncement of the Swamp Rats. "We should'a capped all of them blue balled jug fuckers last year when we had the chance."

They all agreed that it was going to take more than a polite request for the Rats to sacrifice one of their own.

Tank started smirking, and began to laugh. That was unusual enough, but his plan to deal with the Rats was perfect.

"How about we catch a few of those ol' boys and keep them as guests for a while? Torment them sons-a-bitches, keep 'em blindfolded and scared. I can see them now, gather them in the blocks, keep 'em chained like dogs, and wait 'til someone notices they're gone. It shouldn't take long, maybe a week or so."

Burger was rubbing his moustache and thinking. "Easy enough to do, the little fuckers think respect is just a word they ain't heard before. They're always in town causing shit with people. We feed them good while we have them, tell them a man should have a full belly before he gets dead.

They're mostly dopers anyway, won't eat much, 'specially when we slip one or two out of the mix, and his buddies think they got the bullet that's coming to them."

Leech grinned and laughed. "You are some sick motherfuckers, makes me proud to ride with you. What say we go find our first Swamp Rat?"

They got up and headed for the door leaving the table full of empties and a few scattered people wondering what that pack of jokesters were up to.

*****

John left the club and went home to take care of a few things before he went back to the bar. His place was in the middle of twenty acres of hardwoods, rocks, and wildlife. This was his sanctuary when people became too fucking much for him to deal with. Knowing he planned to bring a stranger here made him pause while slapping the clip in his favorite Colt Semi Auto .45 cal. It was an original, and there had been times it had kept him alive since he bought it from an old timer shortly after he got stateside from the Middle East.

"You dumbass, you had to wait and see what she needed. You always have to find where you fit, and you found it, too fuckin' bad you had to drag ass until she'd been hurt to man up." Berating himself just added fuel to the deadly thoughts he was having. The more he thought, the colder the intent.

He secured the clip and added two extras to his shoulder rig. He'd made it especially for his body, mainly because no one manufactured what he was looking for. The daggers in his boots were checked and the throw down was taken outside to run a round through before going into his saddlebags. He'd hate to leave it behind, it was a sweet little .380, but as far as a weapon for practical use, his hands were way too big to use it comfortably. He had others, but this one he'd already taken it to the grinding wheel and removed the serial numbers. The bullets were wiped clean before he slipped them into the mag. In fact, every centimeter of the gun was clean, no prints.

He looked around the place before he left. The logs were hand hewn and he'd built the entire place almost exclusively by himself. When he needed help, he'd called in a favor from Tank, Baron, Lonnie, and Gunner. They were the only people who knew about this place. He didn't spend much time here, most of the time he lived in the bungalow down the block from the garage.

He mounted up and started hunting. It was six thirty and full dark, but the darkness didn't bother him, he embraced the feeling of wind on his face and it pissed him off that he had to wear the brain bucket required by the law in this state. He was flying his colors and drove down to the state line hang out where bikers from both sides of the state lines bent elbows. There were fights almost nightly, but there were times a man had to feel alive, and at times like that, this was the best kind of place to go for the fight he was looking for.

Tonight he wasn't looking for a fight, he was looking for one asshole, and he would find him, no matter how many fuckers went down between now and then.

As he'd expected, the parking lot was crowded. The place was a dive, but it was clean, and the beer was cold. The bouncers at the door looked close when he walked up and nodded. They nodded back at him, and he entered the darkened room. There was a band tonight situated behind chain-link fencing, and the sight triggered a memory about a band singing behind a fence, with a rowdy crowd throwing everything from vegetables to beer bottles at the fencing.

At first glance, he didn't spy any Swamp Kings and was disappointed. Those fuckers were putting him to more trouble than he wanted to deal with, but once he found them, life was gonna be fucked up for those he picked for fun and games.

He made his way to the bar and signaled the skimpily clad bitch who was flirting with a beefy motherfucker wearing a Burning Bastards cut.

She turned to look at him and he saw she'd been scrapping with someone. The black eye and scratches on her cheek were hard to miss. She came over to him and gave him an admiring look. She got the look that some women get when they were attracted to him. He had to admit she was good at that look, probably got her a lot of tip money to pay for the arnica oil based cream to heal her bruises and wounds.

"Well hello there, big man, what can I getcha?"

Damn, her voice was so high pitched that it almost hurt his ears, the bitch sounded like a cartoon mouse with a lisp. He ordered a Miller Lite and waited for her to give up on enticing him into buying her a drink. She had nice tits, and the butt cheek shorts she wore showed her body enough to entice any man. Fuck, too bad Stevie was stuck in his brain, 'cause this one was right up his alley.

He slapped a five on the bar and turned to survey the room again. This place was worse than he remembered, but it was the kind of place the dregs of society, even the biker community's dregs, came. So far it appeared to be a dead end for tonight. He finished the beer and set the empty down. He waved the squeaky voiced woman away, and made his way to the door.

His next stop was Drain's Watering Hole, and he found pay dirt. Three Rats were stumbling toward their putts, and he rode right up, parking his scoot behind two of the mud crusted bikes. He shut her down and took his time removing his helmet, placing it precisely in the middle of the handlebars over the gages. He swung out of the saddle and stood, stretching his arms out, cracked the kink out of his tensely held neck to loosen it. He turned to face the three fuckers that would be the first to feel his rage. One of the dumbfucks stepped up like a Billy bad ass.

"You need to move the scoot, or we'll have to move it for you, and seeing as how you are the only one of your kind here, you need to do it fast." The dumbass turned to his companions and began to talk shit about the Breed. "This pansy ass motherfucker thinks he can come onto our turf and play, we should show him the error of his ways."

John tuned out what the fool was saying, he was watching their body language to tell him when they made their first move. He saw the one on his left center himself, and knew that he would be the first to come at him. It was just like a typical bar fight, the smallest man in the room always had to try to prove himself. He never got to touch John. The flat part of John's palm connected with the little guy's nose, and blood spouted everywhere. He went backwards and his buddies rushed forward to get their licks in.

John was disappointed at how easy the ol' boys went down. The mouthy fucker got a decent punch in before John broke his arm, but the quiet one actually tried to make it interesting. Unfortunately for him, his Rat brother decided to pull a knife and attempt to rejoin the fight. He came up on John's side, and John barely had enough time to pull his opponent by his cut around to block the blade.

One thing he could say about those boys, they liked to keep their blade sharp. The blade slid home just under the leather cut, and into the man in his grasp's side. It was a fucked up scene to watch, and John shoved the man back into his assailant. The mouth picked up a rock to throw at John, and got a kick to the head for his stupidity.

John was disgusted, not much of a fight, and the three of them should have been able to at least make him work for the pleasure of beating their asses'. Well they were going to be the first examples and he pulled the man that was closest to him to his feet and bashed his rotten front teeth into his mouth, "You boys just keep running your mouths, I'll be happy to show you the wisdom of shutting the fuck up when a man is trying to deliver a message.

"Now that I have your attention, the message is for you to give to the coward piece of shit that hurt my woman. You tell him there is no rock, swamp, or cesspool he can hide in, I will find him." He kicked the bleeding man in the thigh. "Do you hear me, boy?" There was no acknowledgement to his words, so his booted foot met the belly of the knife wielding bastard. "I asked a simple enough question, do you understand me?" Heads bobbed. He loosed the shirt of the man that was still only upright by the strength of the man that kept him there, and didn't bother watching him crumple top the ground.

"You boys might want to make yourselves scarce, any of you standing between me and that candy assed fucker will get something they don't want to fuck with. I don't give a shit who I have to go through to get him. You've been warned, I see you again, no mercy."

He walked away from the three Rats, mounted up, taking his time to secure the helmet on his head before leaving the lot. There hadn't been enough satisfaction in that little scuffle to appease his case of mad.

Stopping at a gas-n-go to fill the tank and take a piss took a few minutes, but he still had a half an hour before Stevie's place closed for the night. He wanted to be close to see who, if anyone, was watching the evening's routine. There was no one in the parking lot at eleven forty-five. That wasn't a big deal. It was a Tuesday night and most people had to work the next morning, or had workweek responsibilities.

He parked his sled behind the building and was happy that she had lights glowing for security. Her Jeep was parked closest to the door, and he was impressed with the small camera he spied under the eave. She wasn't naïve or the type to stand around wringing her hands while a man took care of her problems. He admired that. He recognized she might never need him for any specific purpose again, but if there was a chance he could find a permanent spot in her life, they might make it work out. All he had to do was convince her.

One thing was for sure, he'd been attracted to her for years now, and had done nothing to let her know. He wanted to beat his own ass for being such a chicken shit. If he'd claimed her before now, no one would have gotten the idea they could fuck with her. Even the brain dead Rat fucks.

She knew now, and it seemed she wasn't against the idea. He didn't dare think life-long here, but for now, well, they would have to let time decide.

After a quick hike around the vicinity, he found no one bothering to watch her place but the momma cat that had a litter of kittens in an old plastic bin in the edge of the trees. The pie tin filled with crunchy cat food sitting on top of the dumpster told him that someone knew the furry family was there and was softhearted enough to care for them.

He stepped up to the backdoor and beat his fist on the metal to get someone's attention. The bartender was leaving about the same time, or so he said, and went out to his ratty old truck while John went inside, making sure the door closed securely behind him.

CHAPTER THREE

Stevie was in her office with the door open, waiting for him. She'd seen him on the camera the minute he pulled his bike around her Jeep and parked next to it. She looked up at his big frame coming into her room and felt a flutter in her chest. He always had this effect on her. He was probably six foot four inches tall and built like a centerfold in a Playgirl magazine. She loved the way he moved, the way his eyes narrowed when he was amused. When she first noticed him his head had been completely bald. Since then he'd begun growing the thick dark hair, but kept it almost military short, and it looked sexy on him. The thin line of dark whiskers running along his jawline and moustache over his full top lip intrigued her. Those mossy green eyes looking at her narrowed in amusement, and she felt the blush creeping up her cheeks for being caught studying him. She looked down at the stack of money she'd just counted but couldn't remember what the total was. Thankfully, she'd written it on the deposit slip, or she would have had to take the time to fumble her way through counting the bills over again in front of him.

"I was just about ready to put this in the safe and hit the shower and turn in. As you can see I'm fine here, and as safe as I'd be anywhere else. You've been very supportive, and I owe you an apology for almost falling apart earlier. My brother used to say I needed to toughen up and not be such a crybaby. Shit happens, right?"

She got up and went to the small panel with the safe behind it, clicked the small unseen tab on the bottom of the frame to lift the false dial. She opened the safe and placed the bundle of cash inside, closing it and taking her time to turn to look at him with confidence in her body language. "You can rest easy knowing I'm safe right here in Harry's old room. He didn't have time to get the business up and running and afford an apartment. He put all of his money into the business. You have to go through the supply closet that leads to the room. No one knows about it being there but me, and now you too."

She smiled to let him think she had it under control. She was tough. She was alone, had been violated, threatened, and was scared to death. She was also way too attracted to a man that only showed a token interest in her once he thought she needed him to help. Fuck that, if she wasn't worth spending time with before the attack, she wasn't going to take solace in his arms out of his pity for her now. She'd thought of little else but the kiss earlier today. How could she even think about having sex with any man so soon after the attack? Especially a man who she fantasized several times a week about.

John followed her out of the office watching her check on various things that needed to be checked before she could turn out the lights and leave. He didn't see any reason for her to double check the fuckin' salt shakers.

"You can take all the time in the world you want, but you are coming with me to a place I know is safe. Now, or an hour from now, makes no difference to me. I'll wait."

She shook her head. "John, I am a grown woman, I can keep off the radar for a while until it's safe for me to resume my life. I shouldn't need to hide out like a frightened five-year-old. Deputy Wilson stopped by an hour ago and said he would be patrolling the area more than usual. I'll be fine and if Baron could maybe make a call to the Swamp Kings, he can probably clear up any misunderstanding." She smiled and spread her hands out to her sides, "They would have to be completely delusional to ignore a request from that man."

She was so naïve, but he was tired and they had a ride to take. "Get your purse and keys or whatever you want to take with you, I'll take you to your place tomorrow and you can get the rest of your stuff you might need while Baron's warning sinks into those shine soaked heads. You're the one who doesn't understand and right now I don't want to take the time explaining it tonight."

He stood in front of her, and she clenched her jaws for a minute before shaking her head no.

"Stevie, don't make the mistake of giving me a reason to spank your ass, you have no idea how close I am right now. You need to move your happy ass and stop giving me shit about it."

He waited a heartbeat, then reached for her, but she back peddled quickly and headed for the office. He followed close in case she tried to hide out in the room with the locking door. Not that the lock would have stopped him, but the trouble would just fuel his pissy mood. When the door flew back behind her, he knew his estimate was right. Fuck.

He grabbed her by the waist and sat in the chair he'd occupied before. He had to wrestle with her a little and reached for her arm that was pinching his calf, but she moved at the last second and his hand encountered something even softer than her upper arm. The breast filled his hand and he got sidetracked feeling the hardening nipple in his palm. He rubbed the nubbin on the flat surface of his palm and grinned. His fiery little Stevie was not as opposed to the way he was handling her as she acted.

"There's something about humans that always tell on them when it comes to the sexes. That ridge under your belly is nature's way of telling you that I want to fuck you, and this sweet nipple in my palm wants my mouth to give her some love. We can either give into what nature is saying, or you can get your ass up and leave with me. *Hey, that hurt*."

He didn't get the chance to continue talking. The little witch had bitten his thigh. He let go of her breast and laid his palm down on her ass hard enough to gain her attention and her teeth let go of his denim-clad flesh. She screamed, and he gave her another whack, he added two more before he asked her, "Do you think you can act like an adult now? I'm not complaining, you have the perfect ass for spanking, nicely rounded with enough padding for my hand to bounce back a little each time I smack it."

"Let me go you big asshole, I want you out of here and leave me alone. You come in here after the trouble and demand that I—" He smacked her again. "John, let me up. I don't want to fight with you, we can compromise and I'll show you that I have a safe place already."

If he kept this up he would find out her panties were becoming soaked and any pretense on her part would be just words that he'd ignore. She tried to gather her thoughts and tamp down the excitement she was feeling.

Too late, damn, his fingers were trailing down the seam of her lightweight slacks. His fingers lingered at the spot that felt the wettest and she hung her head. "Let me up, I'll go with you for tonight." His fingers kept running up and down to her clit with a gentle pressure. "John, I... You have to stop that."

"Stop? I don't think so, not yet. You have no idea how many times I wished to have you wet like this. Most of the time my mind had you naked in my arms while I fingered your sweet pussy, but this is reality and I'll let you up when you have an orgasm. Maybe two. I wish there was a bed close enough to lay you down and lick the honey out of your pussy. Thinking about the taste and texture of you is giving me more ideas."

His fingers kept the pace and her pleasure steadily mounted until he kept one finger over her clit and pressed harder while encouraging her to give it up for him. "Come on, sweet thing, you can give it up, I'm here, I'll catch you. Take what you want." He must have felt the way her body tightened just before she fell over the cliff screaming her pleasure.

His fingers were still pressed into the seam of her pants, but she was too tired to do anything about it. She'd had orgasms before, but not like this. He was a Neanderthal, a bossy arrogant asshole, he'd also given her the best orgasm to date. When she got her breathing under control, she told him to let her up.

"Let me get my purse." He helped her to her feet, and stood himself. She was too embarrassed to look at his face, but looking down was a mistake. The hard length displayed behind his jeans was obvious, and her head shot up to look at his face. "I, uh. Do you, uh, want me to take care of that for you?" She didn't know if the idea excited her because she knew she was the one that caused his hard-on, or because she wanted to taste him. Either were legitimate reasons.

He shook his head, "Not yet, maybe when we get to the place we're going. I can deal for a few. Once my pants come off, we aren't going anywhere until we're both too tired to blink."

Okay, that was pretty clear, he planned to get naked with her and, too tired to blink? That might be fun, but why was he suddenly interested? She planned to find out as soon as possible. She picked up her purse and moved toward the door where he stood. "I'll follow you in my Jeep."

They got outside and she headed for her vehicle, but he had her arm and shook his head. He watched her closely as she opened the door and started to hike her leg inside. "Do you really want to test me tonight?" She backed out of the doorway, and bent to put her key under the mat.

She straightened up and glared at him. "I don't like you." His shrug at her words, showing her that he wasn't impressed. "I busted a nail taking the key from the ring, do you know how long it took me to grow these claws out?"

He knew damn well that she didn't have the kind of claws she was bitching about, her nails were blunt cut, and playing the guitar kept them that way. She had small callouses on her fingertips from the strings, so he grinned. "Sorry about that, I'm a mean fucker." He dropped the helmet over her head and secured it, before reaching into his saddlebag and pulling out a turtle shell helmet for himself. It wasn't exactly legal, but the heat usually left him alone at night. They rarely tried to stop a bike after dark around here, period.

He took her off the kickstand and started the engine before jerking his head for her to hop on. She hesitated for a few heartbeats, took a few deep breaths, and lifted her leg over the seat behind his hips. The last ride she'd taken was with her brother, and it was also the day she lost her only sibling. A year ago, he'd dropped her off at the bar and left for a meeting at the Breed's clubhouse. He never made it home. She didn't know he was dead until she saw the police cruiser in front of the bar the next morning, and Deputy Wilson held his hat in his hands as he informed her that Harry was found in Glory Ravine, dead of an apparent single vehicle accident. There hadn't been much for her to bury.

The theory was that he'd lost control of the bike and ran off the road, flipping the bike end over end and bursting into flames, burning Harry's body beyond recognition. She kept looking at the pictures of the accident and later, she'd finally discovered what bothered her so much about the accident. The bike was burned, but there was not a ding or a dent anywhere on the machine. She prayed Harry was faking his death for most of the last year, but came to the realization that someone had killed her brother and set it up to appear to be an accident.

Her ass was numb from sitting on the four by six inch pad of leather before they came to a two track leading into the woods. She held on for dear life and he drove around the potholes and tree roots in the unkept path. He stopped the scoot in front of an oversized log cabin, with a wooden porch complete with a swing, and a raccoon was chewing on something as he sat on the railing.

It was too dark to see much, but the small clearing let the light from the moon and stars illuminate the steps. She tried to pull her leg from the bike, but got a cramp in her butt cheek and grabbed it, attempting to rub out the painful muscle. "Fuck, damn it, fuck, that hurts." She pulled her leg and ended up on her ass in the tall grass for her efforts, with the cramp still keeping her leg taut.

John shook his head at the sight of her half reclining on the grass. *Damn, I should have thought about that.* That pad was mostly for show anyway. It was a fucking wonder that she hadn't been bitching all the way here.

He set the kickstand on one of the flat rocks in the ground and moved to help her.

"Hey, hang on a minute, let me help you, first let's get the brain bucket off your head, it's wobbling around until only half of your face is showing." He removed the helmet and set it on the seat of the bike. She was making such an awful grimace he felt doubly bad for her, and reached for her thigh. He rolled her onto her stomach and began kneading her back just above the cheek of her ass, and down her thigh until he felt the muscles relax. "There you go, I thought you rode before, sorry about that."

Stevie rolled onto her back and took the hand he was extending to her to assist her up. "I used to ride with Harry all the time, I even have a license to ride, but I haven't gotten a bike yet. And for your information, big boy, my brother was considerate enough to have a decent seat on his scoot. Unlike some men I could name that are dumb enough to believe a woman wants to be numb from the waist down after fifteen miles of riding on a thin slice of leather over a metal fender. I should have taken my chances in my Jeep. I'll be lucky if I don't walk bowlegged."

He wasn't about to defend his choice of transportation. This was his personal bike, he knew this baby from the ground up. He should since he built it himself. It had a 1200 Harley motor and he'd given it a little love, making it into a 1500, the tranny came with the motor, but the rest of the bike was strictly John Handy. He had two other bikes at the shop, one was a bagger with the kind of seat she was talking about, and the other was for playing in the mud and rougher terrain.

"Come on, you want to ignore Igor there, he's a bum. I made the mistake of feeding him when his mother was killed up at the highway. I brought him here to turn loose but he was too small to take care of himself so I took him to the shop for Lonnie and Chewy to take care of. Chewy took him home and let his ol' lady and kids take care of it. He'd probably still be at their house raising hell but he bit Chewy and one of the kids. So here he is, back in the wild, he shows up for handouts when he knows I'm around."

He turned around after unlocking and opening the door to invite her in, but she was petting the little shit. Igor was chattering at her and trying to get her to pick him up. She was giggling, and he liked hearing that sound coming from her. "Come on, you can listen to his story of sadness tomorrow, trust me, he's always complaining about something."

He flipped the lights on in the main room of the cabin and she was happy to see that the place was furnished nicely. In her opinion it needed a few splashes of color, but the room was open and she loved the wood paneling. She walked to a painting done in oil featuring a river and trees. It was beautiful. Along beside it were pictures of the same area that the painting depicted.

The furniture was large, leather, and looked comfortable enough to sleep on. She turned to see John taking a beer from the stainless fridge. All in all the open concept of the place was country living, with modern conveniences. She loved it.

CHAPTER FOUR

He didn't ask what she thought of the place, it was his, and he liked it. It would be good if she liked the place, but not necessary for the purpose as far as he could see. From the way she was touching everything and nodding as she made her way around the living room, he felt satisfaction settle in. Her approval was not necessary, no, but knowing that she enjoyed some of his personal touches made him smile.

"The bathroom and bedroom are in back through there," he gestured to the opening in the back wall of the room. "You can find towels and stuff in there."

She had to say something, "I love this place, it fits the setting, and I can see me curling up on that couch to read a good book in front of the fireplace when it's cold outside. I would buy a place like this in a heartbeat if I could afford it. You were lucky to find it. The only drawback I can see would be, not wanting to leave the place to go to work every afternoon."

She walked through the short hallway and opened a door. Thankfully it was the bathroom. Again she was surprised and admitted to jealousy. Lucky man, to own the claw footed oversized tub. The corner featured a glass enclosed shower, but the main attraction was that tub. She promised herself that if she ever could afford a place of her own, she would have one of them so she could "wallow around like a pig in mud" as her brother used to say. She sighed, and began to strip out of her smoke scented clothes. A shower was the quickest way to get clean, and she stepped inside the glass door.

The heat of the water relaxed her and allowed her to let go of most of the day's tension. She rinsed the soap off and reached for a towel, *uh oh, problem*. She stepped out onto the pile of her dirty clothes, and scooted her feet over to the cupboard to snag a large bath towel. She toweled her hair first to get the excess water down to a minimum, her hair was really in need of a cut, but she hadn't taken the time to make an appointment. It was nights like this that she regretted her habit of putting it off. It would take her a while to comb the butt length wheat colored mess. She would just throw a braid in it after detangling it and call it good for the night.

Drying the rest of her body, and looking for the shorts and tank she'd brought to sleep in, reminded her that the clothes were in her bag in the other room. *Damn.* She wrapped the towel around her and tucked the end under her arm. She tried to call for John, but he either hadn't heard her, or he was gone from the house. She walked out of the bathroom with her wet clothes hanging from her fingers. John was nowhere to be seen, but she heard the sound of his voice from out on the porch. She stopped to listen, but his was the only voice she heard. He must be on the phone. That was good. She hurried over to the big couch and bent over to pick up her bag.

The click of the door lock startled her as she was sorting her sleepwear from tomorrow's clothes, and she jerked upright with both hands filled with clothing. Her blue underwire bra dangled from her hand. She could feel the towel loosen, and she squeaked, dropping the clothes in her grasp too late. The towel dropped at her feet, leaving her stark naked with her hands raised midway in the air. She saw John standing three feet away and he was staring at her face, not the obvious places she'd have thought he'd be staring. Once he caught her eye, his gaze lowered and she crouched down quickly to gather the towel around her again.

"I'm sorry, I left my bag out here, I forgot to take it into the bathroom with me." She tried to stuff her clothing back into the bag, and felt him standing next to where she was on her knees. She turned her head and found herself eye to zipper, and her earlier recollection of his thick cock behind denim was proving true to life. She tilted her head further back to see his face, and licked her lips at the sight of pure male hunger on his face.

This hadn't been a scene she'd pictured of the two of them before, but fuck it, she wanted to see this man raw and feel him tremble under her lips. She wondered if his sperm would taste salty or slightly sour. She slowly smiled and reached for the buckle of his belt.

She felt like she was opening a present on Valentine's Day for some odd reason. He wore boxer briefs and even the grey cotton showed his prick off as it stood tall, peeking over the elastic waistband. She leaned in closer and licked the small drop of pre-cum from the dark pink flesh, and heard him draw in his breath. Oh yeah, this was going to excite them both.

She peeled back the material slowly, as inch after inch was revealed, she placed kisses down his length until she got to the spot where his shaft sprung from his furry wrinkled ball sack. Working her way north, this time using her lips and tongue in a sliding suction until she encountered the rough knot of skin just under the flared head of his prick. She pulled that skin into her mouth, sucking strongly and mashing it with her tongue to the spot behind her front teeth and the roof of her mouth. Her hands dug into his ass cheeks and she smiled, feeling the tremble in his thighs. She wiggled her tongue on the skin, turned it loose from captivity and slid her mouth over the head of his prick.

The feel of his hands fisting handfuls of her hair made her moan and him push his cock deeper into her throat. He was too big for her to try to deep throat him, so she brought her hand up and circled the thickness in a tight hold. She used her empty hand to fondle his sac. Long ago she'd learned that pinching the wrinkled skin on a man's balls enhanced their pleasure and she moaned and gave into the urge to give him the best blowjob he'd ever experienced.

She kept movement going on his cock, and there was no denying that his reactions were turning her on. She felt the wetness gathering and sliding between the lips of her pussy. She pushed herself up onto her knees and brought her thighs together to take some of the need away, but that was completely ineffective. She moaned her frustration and felt his thickness begin to throb and pulse. His hips kept time with the spurts of his cum, releasing into the back of her throat. The movement of her throat as she swallowed ramped his pleasure and the last stab of his prick held her throat open and tested her gag reflex, until she concentrated on relaxing the muscles of her throat and neck. She gave the shaft in her hand another few strokes and tasted the small amount of cum that came onto her tongue as his deflating cock retreated.

She sat back on her heels, hands cupping her breasts pinching her nipples, enhancing her own coming orgasm. Her head was tossed back and she began panting, moving her hips. One of her hands slid down her body intending to take her clit to the ultimate conclusion, but his hand got there first.

He shoved two fingers inside of her tunnel while his thumb pressed and worked her clit back and forth, until she cried out and began jerking like a puppet. She felt the thick fingers stretching her and gasped as the second orgasm hit her, causing his hand to become drenched with her juices. His hand pulled her hair, dragging her head up for his open mouthed kiss. Their tongues slid along each other, like lovers sliding their naked bodies in a sensual massage. His fingers untangled from her hair and rubbed her head lightly. He pulled his lips back and touched his forehead to hers.

"That was one of the hottest things I've ever seen or done. Thank you." They sat like that for another minute, and he stood, pulling her to her feet with him. "Come on, let's get comfortable under the quilts."

She made a quick stop in the bathroom to clean up a bit and rinse her mouth. She felt great, but her body was weary. It had been a long day and night. Why she felt shy about walking around nude in the short distance between the bathroom and bedroom made her shake her head. He'd already seen it all, and he hadn't told her to cover up yet, so it was on him if he had a complaint. She entered the bedroom, but he was nowhere to be seen. She chose the side of the bed that was furthest from the door because she was pretty sure that he'd insist on being the first defense if someone were to break in on them.

Harry had been that way as she was growing up. Once their parents went to prison for trafficking and RICO violations, Harry had slipped into the bedroom of the foster home the county had stuck her in, and took her away from the place.

They'd stayed in a few rough places, and Harry always insisted on being closest to the door. Once he got a good job tending bar, things got better. He'd bought the bar with little more than his enthusiasm and talent for chatting up the ladies. Being a full patched member of the Breed hadn't hurt either. They trusted him enough to hold the note on the place, and he'd worked like a dog to build the business and pay the bills. He insisted that she get her GED and at least go to the Community College nearby. He gave her the Jeep for her college graduation, and threw her a party at the bar.

Thinking of Harry, and what she believed happened to him, depressed her, but he would tell her to knock it off. Living was for just that, living. Dead was dead. She fell asleep thinking that Harry would probably like John Handy.

John moved the bike into the shed after pushing Igor off the gauges. His phone chirped again and he shook his head at Leech and the boys. They were the best fuckers in the world for having at your back, but they were also effective cockblockers tonight.

Leech was ripped, and from the background voices, it sounded like he wasn't alone. "Hey, bro, we got a little prezzie for you to play with. It took our little Charming Charm to snag him, but that fucker snapped at her bait and we got him in the net. You, yep, you can see him in the morning, we got him on ice, and tonight, we plan to go fishing some more, just like shootin' dumbfuck chickens in the coop. We're gonna get you a collection, that way, you can pick one each day to send back to his fuckin' hole in the stinkin' swamp until we snag the right one. You betcha, we'll get the fucker and have a damned good time doing it. See ya in daylight."

John pulled the phone from his ear and stared at it. Did they snatch a Swamp Rat and had him in the blocks? He sat on the porch and hung his arms over his spread knees and grinned. Yeah, that was what Leech said. How many blood brothers would go to so much trouble for a man in his situation? Not many, that was for fuckin' certain. Knowing they were actively helping him find the cocksucker who hurt Stevie made him feel good. After the way he'd fucked with Leech and the man sounded like the ringleader of the bunch...he had no words.

He stood and entered the cabin. It felt different with her here, less impersonal. He never noticed the difference before. He locked up and took a quick shower, before climbing in next to the woman who was coming to mean too much, too fast to him.

He'd been attracted to her for too long to convince himself that all he would want from her would be a quick fuck. If the feeling in his chest didn't begin to calm down soon, he would worry that it would never go away. If she didn't have the same feeling, well, he'd be fucked, that's where he'd be.

CHAPTER FIVE

Swamp Kings

The Swamp Shack sat back off the road almost a mile and if a person didn't know what he was looking for, they'd never find the place. That's how the Swamp Kings liked it. It was their group's only clubhouse, and even though they were a single chapter club, they had fifty members that regularly showed up to important meetings and events. They considered themselves 1% ers, and most of the brothers had few ethics to worry about. The only morals they encouraged were the club by-laws, and somehow they made it work.

Turner Dean aka Pappy D was the prez, and his son, Donnie, who was pacing the floor in the small room toward the backside of the building, were talking.

"How the hell was I 'spossed to know the whore had arrangements with those fuckin' Breeds? I ain't never seen a Patch in the place the times I was there. All that goes in there are the young fucks from town looking for some pussy or a dick to swing on. So now the Breed is all up in arms over a little misunderstanding? What the fuck."

Pappy spit his tobacco juice into an old coffee can and nodded his head. "I can see where you'd make such a mistake, problem is, ya dipt yer dick in her, boy. I jest had a little talk to with that sumbitch Baron up there, and he says the line's been drawn. She's a member of the Breed, an her ol' man ain't takin' the violation light like. He wants us to turn the one who fucked her over to him, or he says he's gonna keep fucking the boys up 'til he finds the guilty one.

"Didja see Toad, Vic, and Jumper? If her ol' man's the one who fucked them up, he's gonna put a hurtin' on you." The older man nodded and spit again. "That's a fact, boy, ain't no ways around it. Yer tough, and I'm proud to call you my get, but if the three of them couldn't take him, you ain't got a lot of chance. Jumper says he's a big mutha, dark-haired, and tats, full on badass with death in his eyes. Say he's cold on ready to get revenge. Boy, you cain't reason with a man in that mind."

Donnie shook his head, and drained his can of soda. "Wasn't me that did that one, that was Candle, he likes to have 'em scared when he dips his wick. He was sayin' she was nice an' tight, an' he was planning to make a habit of visitin' her."

Pappy D was secretly pleased his kid hadn't been the one to drop on the split tail, he had plans for Donnie to take over after he was in the ground, and the boy couldn't do that if he was dead.

"We ain't givin' him up, so spread the word to have the boys watch their asses, this big motherfucker's a bad one, and he's got the Breed behind him." Donnie nodded and left the room.

He stepped into the main room of the building and spied Tonda wiping down the long feast table. It was Pappy D's birthday and they were already building the fires outside to make a crab boil. It was the rainy season and normally the pot would be dumped on a table outside for everyone to help themselves to the delicious meal, but the flies and mosquitos were such a bother, that it ruined the festive mood of the partiers. The men had constructed this plank table to keep the food clean from so many bugs.

Tonda's ass kept swaying back and forth, and since she was wearing her denim skirt that never covered her entire ass when she bent like that, he stepped up behind her and gave the generous cheeks in front of him a sharp slap.

"You be'in a tease an I got just what a bad girl like you needs to show her the error of her ways. You want me to give you what you deserve here? Or come back to the room and get more than you asked for? I'm in a mood to play with my food for a bit."

When he'd slapped her ass, Tonda straightened up and turned to face the hairy monster behind her. He was her favorite fuck, and she smiled as she tossed the rag she was using onto the table. "You are so right, Donnie Lee, I am a real bad girl, why I didn't have your dick to suck on for my breakfast and had to settle on ol' Derby to drink from."

Her last words were squeaked as she was taken by the arm and half dragged to the door. Her grin showed anyone watching there was no need for alarm from the way the two rushed through the small crowd of cooks.

Allan and Cord were standing by the dump pile, and seeing them gave Donnie ideas, he jerked his head at them indicating they should follow. Tonda was built to take them all on, and damn sure would before they were finished with her.

She hesitated at the door when she noticed the other two were closing in on them, but decided they must want to talk to Donnie. She wasn't alarmed when he told her to strip, even with the others there, she'd long ago lost her shyness about her body. It wasn't until she saw all three men taking their shirts and pants off that she got the idea this wasn't an ordinary spank and fuck with Donnie. She'd been fucked by two men at once before, but usually she had a few drinks in her and was relaxed enough to take the men in her holes without too many problems. Three men at one time, all of them sober, might prove to be more than she'd ever bargained for.

Donnie liked to play her master sometimes, and she was in the role of his slave. He was giving her that look now, and the idea of being a sex slave to three men made her pussy wet. There was no denying the effect having three good looking men with decent sized cocks was having on her. Her nipples were hard as stones, and she shivered with goose bumps dotting her flesh.

"Get on your knees and crawl to Allan. You're gonna take his dick in your mouth, an' Cord an' me are gonna watch for a while."

She went to her knees and hesitated for a minute, *what in the hell are you doing? Get up and get the hell out of here.* Her inner whore told her to shut up and go for it, after all, that's what she was doing here to begin with, right?

The slap of leather on her ass sent her forward to Allan's cock. Her legs were nudged apart and she heard the scrape of something heavy being pulled across the floor. She took his hard prick into her mouth and felt the other two men grab her by the waist and legs, placing her on her knees with her ass in the air, and the movement of her body caused the cock in her mouth to move past the back of her throat and its thickness cut off her air.

"Don'cha give her reason to bite my prick off, I got my woman that needs serviced tonight, and the bitch gets crazy when she sees teeth marks or tastes pussy on my dick," Allan said.

Donnie laughed but understood what the man was saying. Some split tails couldn't handle the fact that a man had needs. Sometimes those needs didn't happen when she was around.

Her legs were spread wider than before, and her entire slit was exposed to the two men. She drew back enough to take a deep breath before her head was pushed down yet again and again. She was thankful to feel his cock swell and begin releasing his cum into her throat just after she'd taken a breath.

The fingers working her pussy were giving her only enough to keep her juices flowing, while the slaps on her ass were beginning to sting more.

As soon as Allan stepped back from her face, Cord stepped up and told her to make it good, "I won't take much of your time, I've been watching, and slappin' your ass for you so I'm ready." He was more aggressive than Allan had been and held her hair in his fist, shoving her head up and down, all she could do was keep her lips open while he fucked her mouth. He came with no warning, and she did her best to swallow his jizz, but some trickled down her chin and onto her neck.

The two men thanked Donnie then left the room. She turned her head to ask him what the fuck he was playing at. "What the hell, Donnie Lee, you try something like that again, you need to ask." The look on his face cautioned her to wait to give him hell until after he was done with her. After that, she was gonna give his kinky ass a wide berth. She liked kinky, hell, she thrived on a bossy fucker taking control. The need to submit was strong inside her and that was why she went with him every time he wanted her.

The look he was giving her today had her anticipating more than his usual spanking her ass and fucking her. When he kept grinning at her as he duct taped her upper arms at the elbow to her knees, and took his kerchief from around his head to use as a gag and tying it around the back of her head, she was more than a little scared.

"You shoulda' kept your mouth shut you filthy little cunt, I'm gonna lesson you good, and when I'm done, you ain't gonna question your master." He grabbed the hair at the top of her head and jerked her head up.

"You're gonna wish you'd gone to church this morning, whore, cause the good Lord is the only one that's gonna stop me from givin' you what you deserve."

He dropped her head, and stepped around the table that was a good eighteen inches off the floor, to stand behind her exposed body. The feeling of dread hit her and she closed her eyes knowing

Donnie was out of control. That thrill knowing he was a leashed psycho, well that was gone, and in its place was fear.

He used his leather belt like a whip over her back and exposed skin. Her legs and ass got the worst of it, but she screamed behind the sweaty kerchief, feeling like he was gonna kill her. It was the worst beating she'd ever had, and there was no escaping the pain he was inflicting. Usually when Donnie got enthusiastic, she found that spot in her mind to drift to. The way he was stroking that belt in different spots prevented her escape.

He dropped the belt and slapped her ass with his palm. "That is fuckin' beautiful, damned if it ain't. Your ass is as red as a black cherry and twice as tempting for me. Gonna have to fuck it, you might want to relax it, bitch, your cunt's as dry as a fuckin' prune now, and I ain't taking the time to give it any pleasure right now, that'll come after."

He leaned down and she felt his tongue stabbing at her asshole. His fingers on each hand were pulling her cheeks apart and the thumbs were digging into her abused cheeks. He let go and moved away from her for a few minutes and she could hear him rummaging around for something. He came back, and poured something over her ass and into her slit. The maniac laughed while he was doing it.

"That'll make sure your dry ass won't take the skin off my prick." He shoved a finger into her hole and she shrieked, he added a second finger and she got louder, and tried to scoot away from that burning ache.

"I like hearing you making that noise, you just keep on makin' it." He pulled his fingers out of her hole and stuck his prick at the little hole that was puckered tight, trying to keep him out. "Here we go you little slut, you love this as much as I love givin' it to you, your asshole's fuckin' tight, makes my prick want to try to find the bottom of it." He worked his hips side to side to send every inch of his cock as deep as he could get. It took a bit of work, but he laid claim to her asshole and laughed while he drew halfway out, then slammed his hips into her cheeks. "You whore, I can feel you squeezing my prick."

He had to be nuts, she tried to squeeze the thick dick in her ass to pinch that fucker off, but that was not gonna work. Her screams got her nothing but a sore throat and a dry mouth. She could only try to breathe through it around the rag in her mouth and the snot dripping from her nostrils. After a few strokes, the burning pain was replaced by a new feeling, and she gasped, oh fuck, yeah, each deep stroke slid over nerves that she'd never felt before, and she couldn't believe how good it felt when he was deep inside. She was heading toward the strongest orgasm, *oh fuck*, she moaned as white hot fog seemed to take over her brain, and her asshole clenched rhythmically on his prick.

"That's it you dirty slut, you feel it, don't you? I can feel your ass grabbing at my cock. Now you know what a lucky bitch you are, don'cha. I'm ready to hose your ass full of my jizz you dick whore," he yelled as the cum pulsed out of his prick in her tight ass, "fuck this is the best, you ain't never gonna tell me no again, fuck yeah, take every fuckin' drop."

Tonda was shaking from the force of her pleasure and only half of what he was saying registered in her brain. She was busy trying to shove her ass back onto his cock to keep him deep as she finished coming too.

His prick retreated once he'd left every drop of his cum inside of her, and he pulled back enough to see her hole wink at him as it slowly closed. She was still shaking and he slapped her still red ass. They weren't finished, and she was gonna walk funny by the time he let her up today. He went to the small fridge and got a beer for himself and came back to her.

"Now, I'm gonna give you a drink, and you're gonna do what I say, or you'll regret it, you understand me?" Her head bounced up and down, so he loosened the kerchief enough to let it hang from around her neck while he held the beer can to her lips. She swallowed the liquid steadily until he pulled it away from her reach.

She whimpered, but kept her mouth shut. Her ass and thighs hurt like a son-of-a-bitch, and she'd bet he'd left marks on her back too. The ring of her asshole still stung too, but that just reminded her of the pleasure she enjoyed.

He put the can down, and turned her over on the table. He ended up picking her up and lying her on her side before rolling her onto her back and pushing her thighs apart as wide as her bonds allowed.

He was still wearing that grin with the intent look in his eyes, and she wondered what he was planning to do. She glanced down and saw that his prick was still soft, so he wasn't in any shape to fuck her, but she wasn't banking on anything with Donnie's mood today. She got an inkling when his fingers started pushing inside her pussy, and his words confirmed her fears.

"You thought I forgot that you needed to be schooled for being a dick teasing cunt, didn't you? I don't fuckin' forget, bitch. Your pussy is soakin' wet, I bet my whole damned hand would fit in this hole, wouldn't it?" He added another finger and worked her into opening enough for his pinky finger to slide up in beside the rest of his digits. Next he added his thumb tucked under the first two, then pushed steadily while her eyes widened and she rolled her head from side to side. "You like this too, don'cha, you'll be begging for my whole fuckin' hand, bitch, I told you so, it'll happen." His knuckles pushed through fast once he pushed hard and steady enough to open her up, and he loved seeing her legs tremble as he backed his hand up half an inch and steadily pushed it back into place, letting her cunt suck up another inch of his hand. It was fuckin' hot to see her cunt take whatever he decided to give it.

She was squirming around and he was getting impatient to see his wrist hanging from her hole, so he used his free hand to slap her clit. "You better stop that shit, you manage to wiggle my hand out of this hole I'll get a fuckin' baseball bat and shove it up inside your fuckin' cunt, you got that?"

Her nodding head and whimpers assured him that she would behave from now on. He pushed with more pressure and his hand disappeared completely. "I'll be fucked, this is so fuckin' hot, you just wait, I'm gonna fuck this cunt with my fist and you'll squeal like a pig on a spit. So goddamned hot, look at that, my whole damned hand. Ha."

She wanted to kill him, his hands weren't little, and he wasn't being gentle. He was still pushing his hand deeper and she couldn't help herself, she could only lie there and let him fist fuck her. He reached over her hip and grabbed the bottle of cooking oil that he'd used earlier and she closed her eyes. She tried to relax, but the feeling of his fingers wiggling around in her vagina felt creepy, and he kept pulling back, and each time he penetrated deeper, the oil would just make it easier for his arm to shove inside. He poured the stuff over her clit and it ran down to surround his wrist. When his free hand began playing with her stretched clit and the lips of her cunt, she almost came off the table, accidently pushing his hand deeper. He started pumping his balled up fist inside of her body and she groaned and cried out as his knuckles punched at her cervix deep inside. When he rotated his hand, it rubbed her g-spot. That, combined with the clit stimulation almost pushed her over the edge again and he came up over, between her spread thighs, to take one of her nipples in between his teeth, and tongued the hard nub. He let one go and snagged the other to treat it equally as harsh. She started bucking and screaming in pleasure and he pumped his fist faster to give her what she was looking for.

It took a bit of muscle for him to remove his hand, but it was worth it. It was something he'd always wanted to try with a woman, and today seemed like a good day. He used his boot knife to cut the tape so she could sit up proper if she wanted to. She was still lying there staring at him, and he remembered the gag in her mouth. He took it from her mouth and untied the wet material before tossing it in the pile of dirty clothing in the basket in the corner.

He helped her sit up and sat in front of her with a big grin on his handsome scruffy face. She balled up her numb fist and sucker punched him. She didn't try to run, or hit him again. "I've never told you no, Donnie Lee, mainly because I seem to have a soft spot for you, always have, but if you ever do that shit again without telling me ahead of time, so I can try to get a few drinks down to be more relaxed, I won't be around for you to do this shit too. And I happen to know the hangarounds are scared of you, and a couple of the others that even I always make sure I'm scarce when they're here.

"I need to know that you understand me, I'll be gone, and you'll wonder where I went when you can't find another woman to play your games with." She kept her eyes on his and he almost waited too long to acknowledge her warning.

He nodded his head and fingered his cheekbone where she'd hit him a good one. "You know I get caught up in playin' your master, sometimes I forget you got free will to come and go as you want." He gave her a wink, "You got a mean damn way of tellin' a man that he's fucked up though."

He patted her thigh and stood, taking her hand and heading to the bathroom. "Let's get cleaned up and grab a plate of that boil, I can smell it from here and it's got my belly rumblin'."

CHAPTER SIX

John took Stevie to town for breakfast, and she made the comment that her ass was gonna pay for, "Being rescued by my knight riding a black Harley."

John grinned, but resigned himself to getting the bagger out of the garage tonight to pick her up from the bar. It was no hardship, each bike was his favorite in the model years. The pleasure of riding, feeling the wind blow the fog and shit from a tangled brain was priceless, no matter what kind of scoot a man rode. Looking at the rectangle of leather made his nuts cringe, so the bagger it was.

Over breakfast she asked about going to her place. "I can run over to the gun shop and pick up something I can handle easily, and I should be fine tonight at the apartment, you don't have to babysit me every night, I know it's cutting into your time." When he didn't answer her, she looked up and saw his narrow eyed stare. "What?"

"Don't start this shit today, you have a safe place to go and someone to keep you from being hurt again. You want a gun, I'll teach you how to use one, it's a good idea for any woman to own her own protection if she has a need. It's a better idea for a woman to know how to shoot the damn thing. Fear can make you reckless, and owning a gun is no guarantee that you're safe. You plan to keep it in your purse right?" At her nod, he continued. "So what happens if your hands are full? You gonna drop what you're holding and fumble around in your purse for the gun? I can say with complete confidence he'd have you down on the ground with his dick in you faster than you can get the damn thing cocked and pointed in his direction."

She was frowning, thinking about what he said, he hoped she was anyway. In his opinion women should be made to take self-defense classes from the day they could walk and talk at the same time. It would save a lot of lives and trouble.

"Lonnie is picking you up from here to take you to the apartment, and you can grab what you need for the rest of the week. Once he takes you to the bar, he's staying, so you can put him to work, or put him in a corner. He doesn't let you out of his sight, and he's happily married so you don't have to worry about his big ass touching you. His ol' lady would hand him his junk in a blood soaked bag if he so much as looked at another woman with interest."

When Lonnie walked into the diner, Stevie wondered what his wife looked like, because the man was sexy as hell. Tall, beach bum looks with a set of the prettiest blue eyes she'd ever seen. She looked at John's amused smile as she took in the sight of his mechanic.

She laughed, and winked at him. "Are you sure his name's not Ken?"

He shook his head and looked toward Lonnie, "No, he's a Lonnie, you'll figure it out." He made the introductions and walked out to the sidewalk with them. "She gives you the slip, call me, the only place she's by herself is in the fuckin' toilet, you got that?" He didn't wait for a reply, he grabbed Stevie and laid a long sexy kiss on her lips and patted her on the ass. "Be good and don't give the boy a hard time."

He mounted up, put on his helmet, and left them standing there.

Stevie looked at Lonnie, who was looking at the people around them. "Well I guess it's you and me, the boss has left the minions alone. Should we go to his place and short sheet the bed?"

Her companion looked confused and she understood what John had been smiling about. Shit, it was going to be a long damn day.

*****

John headed to visit the cop shop. He wanted a name, and since his garage worked on the cages, the cops considered him friendly. He wasn't a fan of cops since his stint as one of them, but he wasn't a hater either. They had a place and were necessary most of the time. The ones who had their tin god complexes didn't last around these parts.

Jimmy Wilson was sitting at the front desk talking on the telephone when he walked into the place. The man was alright, a little uptight at times, but he hadn't given him any problems, so John treated the shorter man with the respect he gave.

Jimmy hung up the phone and smiled at him, so John nodded at him in greeting, neither man offered to shake hands, the lines stayed drawn in some areas of the relationship between the heat and the bikers.

"What can I do for you today, John? Didn't that hussy, Billie Sue, send the check for tuning up the cruiser?"

John laughed and shook his head. "Yeah, she sent it, that's not why I'm here. I wanted to talk to the Sheriff about the Toy Run we're having in a couple of weeks. We don't want to disrupt the traffic like last year, that ol' boy almost tore a strip off Baron for disturbing his lunch so he could direct traffic."

The two men sat around shooting the shit for almost half an hour before Jimmy brought up the subject of Stevie's attack. He didn't mention her name, just that a woman had been violated this week, and there was an increase in breaking and entering around town. "We got prints, but they come back as a biker from out of the area, he's got a record long as my damn arm and been in and out of one prison or the other since his momma whelped him."

John frowned and tried to look puzzled, "We don't have a lot of brothers that have those talents, Jimmy, you know most of us, hell, we don't sanction violating anybody, you know that too."

The Deputy was shaking his head, "Hell no, man, if we thought he was one of the Breed, we'd be at the clubhouse looking for him. This boy is a bad guy with nothing to lose, 'specially since they finally made that three strikes law. Hang on a minute, I got a name, if he shows up, we'd appreciate an anonymous call."

He walked over to the computer desk and tapped the keys, then walked over to the wall where the printer was sitting by itself, because the building was old and electric plugs were scarce. He pulled the sheet of paper off the tray and came back to the desk. "His name is Burton Chandlehook. He goes by the names Candle and Fuse. No one's seen him on the radar for eight months, since the day he was paroled from Huntsville. He never made it to his first appointment with the parole office."

The desk phone began ringing, and Jimmy shook his head at the interruption, "Billie Sue better get back from her vacation soon, I ain't a damn secretary." He answered the phone and the men exchanged waves and head nods. John left the office, and felt the satisfaction of knowing the name of his prey. He wasn't worried about Deputy Jimmy knowing that he knew the name. Coincidences happened all of the time, and proving shit was hard when there was no evidence.

He headed southeast, anticipating the hunt and focusing on his main target. The ride would be a long one, but the information he needed would be worth it, and if he happened to run across a Rat or two, the trip might be entertaining at least. He was doing recon for now, unless opportunity came knocking.

Arkansas had some beautiful countryside, he had to give them that, and the foothills of the Ozarks had a few breathtaking views that he enjoyed seeing on his trip, too bad he didn't have the time to fully enjoy them.

When he stopped for gas and to walk the kinks out, he admired the setting of the gas station and convenience store. The trees and wild flowers looked like a picture postcard.

The cashier was a chatty little guy who appeared to know everybody and everything going on in the area.

"If you're a drinking man, you should know the next county is a dry one. You cain't buy nuthin' but rubbin' alcohol there, so if you're headed home, might want to grab yourself a six to take with you."

John shook his head and walked back to the cooler to grab soda. All he'd need would be for the chatty fucker to keep talking, soon enough he'd get some sort of direction to find the Swamp Rat's nest.

Two people walked into the station, and one started giving the little man shit while the other came around the corner of the aisle to the beer coolers. John was partially hidden on the opposite side of the aisle and pretended that he was looking at the chips. It didn't take long for the trouble to start, and he waited until the two tough guys had the kid hanging over the counter with one of them lying over the top of his scrawny victim while he pulled cigarettes out of the dispenser. His companion was selecting the type of whiskey that they wanted to take with them.

Sure enough, the fuckers wore Swamp King cuts, but they weren't fully patched, that disappointed him, but they would work to further his purposes.

"Hey, boys, now that ain't a nice thing to do to someone smaller than you are. Your big ass is squishin' the little guy. I'm sure he'd co-operate with you stealin' from his place of business, you don't need to be hurtin' him. Why don't you just steal what you can carry and let him go?"

It was all an act, a good ol' boy trying to be helpful to the distressed clerk. The Rat straightened up from on top of the boy and the other jumped down from the counter where he'd been standing.

Typical behavior, they were going to gang up on him for interfering with their fun. *Fuckin' Rats.*

"Well, well, what have we got here, Willie? Looks like a bad boy biker, but you ain't bad 'nuff for the Swamp Kings? Is that why you ain't wearing our colors? What the fuck is a Lucifer's Breed anyway. I'll tell you, a Lucifer's Breed is one ugly motherfucker, that's what you are. You a pussy man, ain'cha?"

Willie kept bobbing his head up and down while the long-haired punk talked. If he wasn't reaching for a weapon, John would have laughed at the expression on the freckled face. His hand held a pig sticker from his boot, and John had all of the incentive he needed by law. He was unarmed, but played the scene up for the security cameras that were located in every corner of the room. He held his hands out to his sides and shook his head.

"You boys should just leave, if you come at me with that toothpick, I'm gonna think you intend to do my body harm, and I'm trained to hurt you if I have to." He knew his words would make the overconfident assholes laugh—he counted on it. Too many Kung-Fu movies instead of cartoons must have been what they were raised on.

"OOwee, we got a real bad assed muthafucker here, I'm skeered, ain't you skeered, Mel?" Willie must've found his voice when he got his weapon in his grasp.

Now all he needed was for them to come and get him before he schooled the punks. It took maybe five seconds for him to break the wrist that held the knife, and another ten to shove the little fucker's head into the metal doorframe. Mel tried to jump him from behind, and John sidestepped at the last second, Mel landed on top of his pal who was now bleeding from a head wound and moaning, while his prone body was blocking the exit.

Like any other Rat would do, Mel tried to yank Willie out from the doorway, but John grabbed him by the back of his shirt and shook him. "You move him, and he might die, that's on you, asshole."

The little prick reacted to that just as John figured he would, he started swinging his fists. He was allowed one knuckle crunching punch, before John punched him in the gut, and as he went down, rather than the traditional upper cut to the jaw, John brought the side of his hand down on the boy's collarbone, halfway between his neck and shoulder. Mel was hauled over to where Willie still laid bleeding.

John walked back to the cooler, got his soda, and came back to the desk to see the clerk watching him with eyes widened. He looked like a fish gulping for water. "Sorry about the mess, here's a twenty to pay for the disinfectant and the soda." He leaned in closer to look the boy up and down. "Did they hurt you?"

The little guy shook his head and rattled his brains enough to speak. "Oh man, that was so cool, where'd you learn to do that?" He offered his hand for John to shake and a friendship of sorts was formed.

"Shouldn't you call the cops or an ambulance or something?" John wasn't surprised when his new friend who introduced himself as Tyler Butler, shook his head.

"Last time they came into the place and my sister called the law, they cut the hoses on the gas pumps and shot the windows out. We usually let 'em steal whatever they come for and be done with it. I haven't had to meet these two before, and I'm not sure what to do with them. This ain't the first time we've been robbed mind you, but usually they don't try to hurt any of us.' He glanced over to where the two men were lying in the doorway. "That one, he's bleeding pretty bad."

John went to the back corner of the room and called Baron. Once he'd related what went down, he asked him if he'd call Pappy D and tell him to come get his boys. "I'll put them in the bed of their pick-up. Thanks." He ended the call, not wanting to get into any in-depth conversation with the prez right then.

He went to the door and started moving the wounded men out of the way enough that he could drag them back out the door and over to their beat to hell and back pick-up. Mel was groggy and in pain, but he was awake, so John gave him the speech that he'd be repeating to every Rat he would find until he had Candle in his grasp.

"You tell Candle to drag his stinking cowardly ass out of that putrid swamp he lives in, and come face me, or more of you boys are gonna suffer until he does."

He went back inside and finished getting the information he sought from Tyler, then he offered the kid a smile and made his request.

"I want you to give me the security footage from the cameras, and don't bother to tell me you don't have access, I just saved your ass, and I want to be able to prove it."

Now that he knew where the Swamp Kings clubhouse was located, he could do some recon before he left the area.

*****

Pappy D came stomping out onto the back porch and started yelling for Donnie Lee. "Get your ass down to the county line station and see what kinda shape those two gator baits has got themselves into now. I jest gotta a call from that Breed bastard, his boy done fucked up Mel an' Willie."

The old man was so pissed he was trembling with his anger, and Donnie was concerned Pappy D would blow a blood vessel or something, but he nodded his compliance and headed for his scoot. He wasn't surprised when the old man called after him to hurry his ass up. Mel was Donnie's youngest brother, and spoiled as they came. He was always having to drag the little bastard out of trouble.

He'd no sooner mounted his bike than Mel drove up in the pick–up, almost running into the line of bikes in front of the club. He slumped over the wheel with the motor still running, and Donnie grew alarmed.

He pulled open the door and reached under his brother's chest to turn the key off, and then pushed Mel upright so he could see what the damage was. A couple of scrapes in his little brother's face wasn't enough to do the damage that Mel must have to be throwing up blood like he was doing.

He laid his hand on the horn to get the attention of whoever was inside the club, and heard screaming from the back of the truck. "Oh fuck me, we're gonna have to call the medics for this one."

Pappy D was trailed Kermit and Dell coming out of the front doors of the clubhouse and almost shoved the two out of his way when he saw the truck. He heard Donnie calling for an ambulance and knew it must be bad. He could hear Willie screaming that his head was split in two, but his concern was for his boy.

"Lay him on the seat, and give him a few sips of water, but nothin' else, if'n he's pukin' blood, there ain't much we can do."

Tonda, Dolly, and June brought the bottles of water and damp towels to try to make the injured men more comfortable. A plastic bag filled with ice cubes was placed directly on top of Willie's head wound that still seeped blood down his face, and Pappy D sat on the steps with his head down, thinking.

He called Donnie over to him, and quietly told him to find Candle. "You bring that troublemakin' sumbitch to me. You do it friendly, or you do it not so friendly, but you bring that fucker here to me, you hear me, boy?"

Donnie nodded his head. Candle should never have been allowed back into the fold when he got out of Huntsville. The code said he paid his due and was one of them, so he was welcomed back with a party and everything. Since he'd been back, they'd had nothing but trouble coming their way, and with the case of mad Pappy was wearin', the shit was gonna splatter the walls real soon.

"I'll go soon as the medics get Mel and Willie in the meat wagon. Mel kept sayin' the one that fucked them up was a big mutha, and said he was lookin' for Candle."

It occurred to him the Breed's prez acted like a decent sort considering, but he wasn't going to say that out loud. Pappy D wouldn't have bothered to call his enemy to send them to help their brothers. Mayhap the Breed was touched in the head kinda like Willie was. If that was the case, then how in the hell did they get to be such bad motherfuckers?

*****

John watched the scene play out in the dirt parking space in front of a weathered old building. None of the men looked like the picture in the mug shot he'd seen on the print out on Deputy Jimmy's desk.

He backed into the trees and hiked to the spot he'd left his bike. He had a long ride ahead of him, but now that he had a location, he'd be back real soon.

CHAPTER SEVEN

It was a long damn ride back to Juanita, but he was focused and ready to kick ass by the time he pulled into the lot at the club. He'd stopped by the garage and traded his daily ride for the bagger so he wouldn't have to make another stop. Gabe and Chewy had everything in order at the shop, so he was free to take care of personal business. He walked in the door and Myrtle told him that the prez wanted to see his ass pronto. As she put it, "You are in trouble, my man; if he has to come get you, me an' Burger are selling tickets." She smiled sympathetically and popped the cap from the longneck she handed to him as he strode past.

He rapped on the door and turned the handle, before walking into the room. Baron was going through the books with Orin and Fingers. When he saw who walked in, his eyes narrowed and he told the number crunchers to get their shit straightened out. "I'm no accountant but I can see we have a problem, you two are in charge of the books, I'm getting the idea that one or both of you are getting ready to make a move. Probably to some place a bike can't find you, but Tank and his accountants are at your place going through the computers there and the office. If he doesn't find a discrepancy, we're good, if he finds that we have reason to worry, we're not so good.

"While they're working, you boys are our guests right here at the clubhouse. If you try to leave before you get the go-ahead, you won't be here as guests, you get me?"

Sweat dotted Fingers's forehead, and while Orin appeared calm on the outside, Baron saw the man kept swallowing. Fuck, he knew they'd been skimming money. He kept a record of every transaction the club made, one set of books was legitimate business, and the other not so legitimate. These two thought they were smarter than the rest of them, they would pay for their error in judgment.

Skids and Burger escorted them from the room while John waited for the ass chewing he had coming. He didn't have long to wait. Once Baron put the bogus ledgers to the side, he folded his hands on the desk and stared at him. John waited him out, there was no point in denying that he was guilty of a couple of minor indiscretions, the phone call was a spur of the moment thing, even if he had reason to hang up on Baron at the time.

"So, this is what I want from you, and don't give me any shit, I've been buried in a damn sty of it all fuckin' day. That phone call just got the ball rolling so tell me why I shouldn't kick your ass from here to the corner, and make it one of those in-depth stories, the kind where I get all the information, not just the fill in the blank version. You know I've got your back, but this shit is getting real close to a war with those gator lickers. Leech and the boys started a collection for you to pick from to get the information you want, and I had to discuss the issue with them today when I saw guest number two coming through the blocks, followed by Charm driving right up to the door a half hour ago and popping the trunk."

He watched John carefully, readying himself to grab the man when he gave him the news.

"One of those boys you fucked up was Pappy D's youngest, and it appears that you weren't the only one who went off the rez today. Our Miss Charming snagged one of the Rats by flattening her tire on the side of I-30 about two miles out of Murky Carl's gator farm. He was real nice to Charm and changed her tire, and when he put the flat in her trunk, he got tasered in the neck for his troubles." He had to smile as he remembered his astonishment when he saw what she'd done.

"She says she owes you for something, and it's just her way of paying you back. You owe the club a roll of duct tape, she used the whole thing wrapping him up to keep him from 'getting himself all upset.' What she didn't know, is that her fish is the biggest one of the bunch aside from Pappy D, she scored his oldest boy, Donnie Lee Dean. They say he's slated to be Pappy's replacement, so it appears I'm not the only one who has your interests at heart. Now talk."

John didn't know what made him sit back down in the chair that he almost jumped out of to get his hands on the fucker in the blocks. Instead of running out to the back, he began telling Baron every detail of the past few days, and concluding with his self-assessment.

"I had to wait until that cockbite son-of-a-bitch hurt her before I could grab my balls and admit that I can make my own spot in her life. She's not buying it yet, but she will, once I have the time to convince her I'm sincere.

78

"I'll teach her how to protect herself, but she's scared of the fucker, and scared people make last second hesitations. I have a big hate going on for him, he violated my woman, and there's no rock he can hide under that I won't find him."

Baron could see that John was as mad at himself as he was at the fuck that hurt Stevie. He remembered the way he'd felt about someone hurting Stretch. Just thinking about that shit made him want to kill the dead fucker.

"We have a problem here, I can't let you hurt Donnie Lee too much unless we get a club vote. You know this, so think about what you plan to do with him before you go off on the man. I'm not looking for an affiliation, I'm happier than hell when they stay in their swamp, but they made gestures last year when Jean Lefore tried to pull his shit. Mostly because they would just be cannon fodder in the middle. They had enough sense to reject that South American drug peddler. We were the lesser of evils."

John remembered, it had taken most of the smaller clubs and both the Bastards and Lucifer's Breed to send those fucks away from the tristate area.

He nodded at Baron, and the men shook hands before John left the room to make a visit to Donnie Lee Dean.

*****

Donnie was cursing the split tail that suckered him. If he ever got the chance, she was gonna get exactly what she deserved, and he would enjoy every minute punishing her for daring to fuck him over. That skinny ass of hers was gonna feel his whip, and he entertained himself with fantasies of slapping her generous tits until she screamed and begged him to stop.

He should've known better than to believe a beautiful woman like that driving a baby blue Camaro from the early 70's was harmless, but that car was fuckin' cherry. The woman was long legged, and bending over the trunk trying to get the spare tire out wearing ass cheek baring shorts and a cropped top that her tits were spilling out of as she straightened up when he stopped to help her. She was tall and long limbed, and thinking of the way she would thank him made him smile and drop right into her trap.

The spot on his neck where she'd laid that fuckin Taser itched, and the duct tape sticky shit was tangled in the few hairs left on his damned arms once that big motherfucker they called Skids had sliced through and then peeled the shit from his body. Skids, and two other fuckers named Leech and Burger, replaced the duct tape with steel cuffs and leg irons. He was currently leashed to an eyebolt secured in the cement floor of a room that was constructed of blocks. There was a bucket in the corner for him to do his business or take a piss. At least they left his hands cuffed in front of him.

The bastard Burger had told him, "I'm cuffing you in front, 'cause I ain't holding your pecker for you to take a piss, and I ain't planning on spoon feeding your ass either. Try any stupid shit and you won't like what happens. You ain't gonna take my advice to heart, 'cause you Swamp Rats just don't learn easy, but when John gets here, you might want to tell him what he wants to know, it'll save you some teeth and a whole world of hurt."

The asshole smiled then, and said "Hell, boy, it might save your life. Did you know our boy was a Ranger in the Army? If he has to head back south, who knows who might be in his path to the fucker that you fools are protectin'."

He shook his head and laughed as they heard a door slam and a man scream. "You don't happen to know a Rat by the tag of Sonny Paulson? Nah, you wouldn't know him by his scream now would you? Swamp Rats squeal when they're hurt don't they?" He laughed as he shut the door behind him, leaving Donnie behind to deal with his thoughts.

Thinking about fuckin' that bitch up just made his dick hard, and he didn't want his jailers to see him sittin' here in cuffs with a hard-on. They might get the wrong idea, and that wasn't something he wanted to deal with.

Aside from his miscalculation in picking that bar on the state line, the rest of this shit was all Candle's doing. He was tired of the entire thing. He couldn't give Candle up, not without a world of shit coming down on his head. So he came up with a plan that should make everyone happy.

By the time the door opened again, he was prepared for just about any scenario. He'd been hearing the screams coming through the door for the past two hours, and it sounded like they were doling out pain to Sonny slowly over time. He wasn't a close friend of the brother, but Sonny hadn't done anything to deserve this kind of shit that he knew of either.

A big motherfucker walked into the room and he held the door for the one called Skids to carry in two chairs. The big fucker had to be John. The chairs were set down in the middle of the room, and Skids left them alone.

John sat in one of the chairs and pushed the other one toward Donnie. "Sit." Donnie shrugged his shoulders and sat. Whatever happened, he was ready, at least that was what he told himself. He was surprised when the man pulled two cans of beer from his pocket and handed one over to him. He didn't know what this fucker was up to, but he was powerful thirsty, so he popped the top and took a couple of draws on the ice cold liquid before John began to speak.

"Okay, Donnie Lee Dean, it's like this. I want the cowardly motherfucker that got his rocks off on frightening and violating my woman. I can say with confidence that I could beat you until you'd need some poor hag to wipe your chin and sing you nursery rhymes, and you won't give your brother up." He popped the top of his own beer and swallowed a good portion of it, and continued.

"I understand you happen to be Pappy D's kid, and are the heir apparent to the leadership role of the Swamp Rats. Don't get that pissed look either, you want my fuckin' respect, boy, you gotta fuckin' earn it. From everything I've seen and heard, there isn't one of you worth the cost of the bullet it'd take to shoot you with.

"You look surprised, but your club is a fuckin' disgrace to legitimate clubs, it's not respect or fear that has kept your people from being allowed to patch over to other clubs. Any club with any common sense knows better than to trust one of you as far as we can see you. If you lazy bastards can't steal it, you sell poison to kids, and threaten until you get what you want. Not a man in your group actually works for a living, and your women are pregnant all the fuckin' time providing you all with welfare checks and food stamps.

"Your fuckin' litter mate was beating on a boy who was working in his family business to earn his way through college when I stopped him. That brain dead fuck that was with him was real brave with a pig sticker in his hand." He drank another swallow, attempting to keep his temper in check. "I don't understand your way of life, and I don't want to. I've earned every fucking thing I own, and so has every man in the Breed."

The mad inside John was too much for him to handle, so he stood and grabbed the chair he'd been sitting in, and hurled it with every bit of strength in his arm. The chair splintered on the wall, breaking into pieces. The big man threw the can in his hand behind it for emphasis, and began to pace.

"You'll be taken care of while you're our guest, I'll have you moved across the hall, but you will be with us until I either find that cocksucking coward, or your daddy turns him over to me."

John stepped close enough for Donnie to attempt to slug him, but Donnie wasn't taking that bait. The man put his finger in his face.

"You're gonna call your daddy and tell him for me that I don't plan on killing the fucker in his sleep, he'll get a fair fight, and if he can walk away when it's over, he'll be free to go. If he keeps hiding, I won't be too picky where he is or who he's with, as long as he isn't moving by the time I'm done. You get me, boy?"

Donnie nodded his head, and decided to try reasoning with the crazy fucker. "I was on my way to get Candle when your whore waylaid me. Pappy D wanted to talk to him about the situation. I think he was planning to cut him loose from the Swamp Kings. He's been more trouble than he's worth for a while now, so don't think your issue is the only one. If you wait a few days, maybe a week, he's fair game for you."

John wondered if the man actually believed a slug like Candle would just peacefully walk away from his hideaway without doing damage. What the fuck, why should he bother trying to explain a damn thing to this kid, no matter the boy had to be close to thirty, he wasn't a man yet, maybe that's why those ignorant fucks acted like they did. None of them grew up.

He pulled his cell phone out and asked for Pappy D's direct number.

"Is this Pappy D? Who am I, well I'm the man who has your boy here, and you get him back once I get what I want." The old man was shouting endearments at him and he smiled. "If you keep that kinda shit up, I won't let him talk to you. Really? Name the place, I'll be there, you want to think you're man enough to cash that check your mouth's

84

writing, I'll be happy to oblige. Now that you have that out of your system, I'm gonna show you what a reasonable man I can be."

He handed the phone to Donnie and waited for the younger man to finish staring at him while he talked to his father.

Donnie ended the call when he finally said, "Yeah, me too, Pappy," and handed the phone back to John. "I guess you gotta do what you gotta do, man, I can't help you and you know it."

John nodded and walked out of the room.

Donnie was asleep in the chair when Skids and another man that he didn't recognize came in and led him into a different room. It was small, and had a toilet in the corner, a sleeping mat was on the floor, and a bare light bulb hung overhead. His leg irons were exchanged for a single ankle restraint, but the cuffs on his wrists remained.

CHAPTER EIGHT

Stevie was learning how to deal with having Lonnie around, and she could see why his wife had him on a short leash too. He was pretty much clueless about women stalking him through the grocery store, and the chickie babes in the bar almost begging him to come with them to a private party, even when one drunk on her ass woman stuck her hand down in his pocket with her address and phone number on a folded napkin.

"You don't have to look at them like that, Stevie, I'm glad that my looks can make them happy. My wife says I'm like a picture in the museum, it belongs to someone else, so please admire, but don't touch. Her name is Sharon, I love her, and she'll never have cause to worry about my loyalty. She knows how some women react when I'm around. When we first met, I was a real horn dog. I thought she wasn't pretty enough to be my woman." He shook his head with a tiny smile on his perfect lips, and continued with his story.

"We were at the same club one night and I was too drunk to drive home. My dates had left because I was more obnoxious than usual that night, I guess I ran them off being the asshole like they called me." He laughed outright, causing the people close to them to turn and stare at the sight of the gorgeous man whose laughter made them smile, wishing they knew what was so funny.

"Sharon tried to stop me from getting on my scoot, and I acted like a real jerk. Long story short, she followed me to make sure I got home in one piece. I ended up wrapping my bike around a yellow pine tree, and she kept me alive long enough for the medics to get there. Next thing I know, I'm awake, but no one knows it but me. I heard Sharon tell John and Gunner that I was too stubborn to die. She said I still hadn't fucked my way through the southern states single party girls yet, and they should know I would crawl off my deathbed to get to the mirror. As long as a woman didn't mind being used for five minutes and told to leave afterwards so I could crawl to the next hole to stick my dick in. I'm sure you get what I'm saying.

"I watched as my friends, and a woman that I wouldn't have screwed, no matter how drunk or high I might be, laughed and made jokes about me. I can admit I was hurt and pissed that everyone thought I was so shallow, but right about the time I'd get a full head of steam on, someone would tell yet another story with me as the comic relief." He grew quiet for a few minutes, remembering the humiliation of hearing his actions being hashed and rehashed.

The women that came to see him always commented on his wasting body, cried and verbally stated how repulsive he looked lying there. There had been only one woman that stayed with him through all of those months of hell. He was locked inside of his body and brain, his own personal Hell, with no way to communicate with the outside world. Without her voice telling him to get his lazy ass up and out of that bed, the sluts were wearing widow's clothes and covering up their boobs when they came visiting, he would have gone insane.

He remembered hearing her cry herself to sleep night after night while sitting in a chair next to his bed, holding his hand and praying to God that he would wake up, "In one piece." There was so much more to his story, but that was none of anybody's business but his and Sharon's.

"If they knew I fart and that my feet stink, or I cry like a five-year-old when Old Yeller dies at the end of the movie, I doubt they'd be as impressed. My lady has no reason to worry, and you don't have to get up in arms on her behalf. It took me a while to grow up, but I know who holds my leash, and I'm not complaining."

Stevie felt her eyes sting from hearing his story, and the declaration of his love and devotion to his wife. "Lonnie, that has to be one of the top five romantic things I believe I've ever heard a man say about his wife. You have a beautiful story and I bet she is a beautiful person. I'd like to meet her someday. Bring her around to the bar sometime, would you? She sounds like a woman I'd love to get to know."

Later in the evening, after her performance, Lonnie asked her who she sang to with such emotion. "I almost lost my tough guy image there, lady. I'm betting our friend, John, has something to do with it, but yesterday was the first time I've seen the two of you together for more than you writing a check for repairs on the Jeep.

"He's a good guy, you know. One you can count on to do something when he says he'll do it." He nudged her with his elbow and winked at her.

"Come on, girlfriend, spill your guts, I told you my deal, tell me yours."

It was her turn to laugh out loud. "If I knew exactly what was going on I would tell you. He makes me breathe funny, does that surprise you? I've been crushing on the bossy, bad boy forever it seems. Yesterday was the first time he gave me the time of day, but that was only after he bullied me into telling him what happened to me four nights ago."

Her own words made her question John's actions since then for the hundredth time. "I don't know exactly what his deal is, and I know that sounds dumb, but he's not exactly the kind of man that's easy to read. If I let myself fall down the rabbit hole, and he decides that I'm no longer in danger, where do we go from there? Will he say, 'See ya later, it's been fun' or stick around? I have no idea what's going on, but I'll let you know when I know, how's that?" She held out her hand and they laughed as they shook hands.

She sent Leon home early, and he was not happy about it, but the place was quiet, and Lonnie could tend bar as good as the older man, so it made no sense to keep both of them there for another hour. She paid Leon by the night, not by the hour, she didn't know what his damage was and didn't bother to ask. Leon had been getting a little too friendly, always asking personal questions, and seemingly innocent questions about her brother. She'd shut his line of questioning down at least twice, by telling him that she never talked about her personal life with her employees. He tightened his lips and shrugged her rebuffs off each time, but she wondered if he had an ulterior motive for asking.

Since the night of her attack, she was getting paranoid, second guessing everything, and examining every person she dealt with behaviors. Now that she thought about it, the day she'd figured out Harry's death was not an accident, was the day she began questioning the motives behind everyone's actions or words.

Now, thinking about Leon and his pissy attitude was enough reason for her to lock the doors early. There were no patrons in the bar, so there was no reason to keep the music on and the lights blazing on the neon outside. Lonnie went about closing the bar as if he'd done the job for years instead of one night, and she asked him why he seemed to know where everything was.

He smiled sadly at her, "Stevie, Harry and I were running buddies before he bought this place, we used to be the big dicks, letting the chickies' chase us down and have their way with us. I remember when he brought you to the area, and how he used to brag about his super smart little sister. I worked here until my accident, and once in a while I'd still fill in for Harry when he needed a break after I got back on my own two feet." He looked away for a second, "I was kind of surprised to see that Leon is working for you. After the way Harry showed him the door, but well, not my business." He set the clean draft glass in the line with the rest of them.

"Wait, what do…are you saying Leon wasn't working for Harry when my brother died?" When he nodded, she narrowed her eyes and clenched her fists. "That miserable son-of-a-bitch, I came to the bar three days after the accident and he was here trying to get his key to work in the backdoor. He told me he worked for Harry. He wanted to make certain everything was still okay here. He told me he needed to clean the fridge and pack up the booze and stuff since the place was closing.

"I wasn't here much at the time, I had a job with Brown & Benjerman as a paralegal. I didn't know."

She thought about that conversation, and his surprise when she told Leon she planned to keep the place if the mortgage holder would allow her to take over the note. She'd been so lost at the time, and offered to allow him to keep working at the bar when she took it over.

"Why did Harry fire the man?"

Before he could answer her question, there was someone pounding on the backdoor, so he went into the office to see who it was before opening the door for John to enter.

The men were talking quietly as they returned, and she compared the two side by side. *Really, Stevie?* There was no comparison. They had height in common, as far as looks went, and that was about it. Though there was also the glaring wet-a-girl's-panties fact that they might be totally opposite, these men were sexier than hell. She preferred John's tough guy appearance over Lonnie's centerfold sex god looks, but for all intents and purposes, neither man would need to do much talking to get a woman to wet her lips and hit her knees.

John felt the weariness leave him when she smiled in welcome. He'd carried a picture of that smile in his mind for the entire day, and seeing it in front of him was even better.

Lonnie clearing his throat brought the two out of staring at each other with heat.

"I was just telling Stevie here that Harry fired old Leon a week or so before he bought it. He was dealing out the backdoor, and from what Harry told me, it wasn't a few ounces of weed. I only mentioned it because after seeing the old fox in action tonight, he's still got his game on."

She had envisioned Leon embezzling money, selling drugs from the bar was even worse. "He's been asking some personal questions lately, and I've had to put it pretty blunt that I wouldn't discuss my family with employees. He wasn't happy when I put it that way, but he dropped it for a few days and I found him snooping in the office last Monday, so if he's the one that killed Harry, how come he's asking so many questions and snooping around?"

She got up from her seat at the bar and started walking around the room. John figured she was worried and needed to get rid of some of her feelings in moving around. He told Lonnie that he could go. "Pick her up in the morning at the diner."

Lonnie said good night and she waved at him from the other side of the room. The puzzle of her brother's death finally fit, but why didn't the police investigate his death when she'd brought the pictures to them from their own files, and said that something was wrong. They'd dismissed her concerns completely.

First thing tomorrow, Leon would learn that she was not as stupid as he thought she was, nor as helpless as she'd been acting. Harry had done his best to give her a normal life once he got a steady job and they had their first apartment. He insisted that she become like other girls her age and took her jeans and leather jacket away. He never allowed her to know his friends, and until the last few months of his life, he'd discouraged her from even stopping by the bar after work.

Later she realized he hadn't wanted her to become a tough biker chick, he wanted her to have a professional husband and a couple of kids, and living in a suburb making her happily-ever-after with the attorney or doctor hubby. His plans for her were written in his journal. She hadn't known he kept one to begin with. She found it in a box under his bunk with skin mags covering the slender book. Reading his thoughts about the death of their parents, and how worried he'd been about her had made her break down and grieve his loss. She never wanted him to feel like a failure, or less than the wonderful loving brother that she knew she could count on to always be there if she needed him. Now it was too late for her to tell him she loved him, or anything else, and she was mad.

Leon had reason, opportunity, and plenty of motive for killing Harry, and she was going to make that bastard pay. She looked toward John who was drinking a beer and watching her.

"If you have a few minutes to wait, I'd like to run something by you, maybe you can help me gather my thoughts about something." She perched herself on the stool next to him, and gathered her thoughts.

"After Harry's death, I had so much on my plate that I never questioned whether the accident was legitimate, I didn't question the bag of ashes they gave me and told me that his body had been burned beyond normal procedures, and the coroner had declared that he died of an accidental death.

"I admit, I was stupid, it never occurred to me that officials would lie to me, or try to cover up the death of a biker. Six months after his death, I opened this report I had requested, and saw the pictures of the accident scene. No matter which angle I looked at the wreckage, I couldn't see a ding or a bent fork, there was no exploded gas tank either. It showed his plate very clearly, but I have studied that picture for over a year, and I still don't believe it was an accident. When I went to the police, I was shuffled from one deputy to another until Sheriff Lime told me to stop trying to make Harry's death into more than it was. He all but banned me from the station and recommended that I see someone to "unscramble" my brains on the subject.

"My question to you is this, Leon was dealing drugs from the bar, and Harry fired him for it. Harry dies in what I think are questionable circumstances, and Leon shows up at the bar acting like nothing had happened, as if he was still an employee. Going by logic, not emotional distress, would it be reasonable for me to suspect that Leon killed Harry, dumped the bike, then set fire to his body and bike to cover up his murder?"

John nodded his head, but he was on shaky ground here, so he agreed with her, after all, her thoughts were similar to what had actually happened, loosely, but her theory could also work to satisfy her questions.

"In theory, I guess it would be reasonable to assume what you're thinking, but proving it is another story. All you have is hearsay evidence and that isn't going to cut it."

He stood and turned the seat she sat on to face him while he ran both hands through her hair. "I thought about you all day, the way you taste, the generous way you give me your body, right down to the way your pussy squeezed the cum from my prick this morning. It's kept me simmering for more all this time."

Switching gears from the murder of her brother to the memory of last night's activities took a few seconds to shift, but the way he was kissing her lips, tugging her head back for deeper kisses, soon put everything else on the back burner. He smelled so good, and his kiss promised more than she'd expected. If she read them right, he was promising a night of satisfying sex, and if last night was any indication of how this could go, she would sleep like a baby when they were done. No nightmares for two nights in a row.

She was almost looking forward to sleeping in his arms more than the sexual release, feeling secure and... Loved would be stretching it, but whatever those feelings were, she'd known she could trust him. His way of waking her up this morning had iced the cake for her.

Her hands went exploring under his cut and found a hardened nipple covered by the soft cotton of his t-shirt. She scraped her fingernail over the tip, and he flinched, so she did it again, and he drew away from her just enough to grab her hand and bring it up behind her back.

"You keep that up, and I'll slide your ass up on this bar and take my refreshment from your sweet pussy, after I spank your ass for tickling me."

She laughed at his threat, not because she didn't think he'd follow through, but knowing she'd found a chink in his bossy armor. "Oh come on, you'd spank me for making you laugh? That's not nice. So if I was to," she leaned in close and latched her mouth over the nipple closest to her and held the small circle in between her lips while her tongue lapped at the tiny bud through the thin material.

The hand cupping her head encouraged her action. "Harder, use your teeth, yeah, like that."

She let go of his nipple after worrying it until he moaned, and gave his crotch a playful pat. "I think you're happy to see me." She started to walk back to the office to get her backpack, and giggled when her arm was grabbed and she was lifted up onto the end of the bar on her belly. She pushed up with her arms, and got a slap on her ass for her trouble. She was still laughing until the third swat. "Hey, biker man, that stings." The forth and fifth smack got her the satisfaction of knowing she'd kicked his thigh in reflex as the intensity of his swats increased.

The waistband of her skintight leggings was peeled down over her ass and thighs, and she felt his lips kissing the reddened cheeks. Somehow she ended up on her back lying on the hardwood surface of the bar with her ankles together and her thighs spread wide. John's hands were trailing up and down the inside of her thighs.

"This is such a pretty sight. Tell me, Stevie, how many orgasms do you think I can give you in the next half hour or so?"

She knew that wicked grin on his sexy lips, she was in for some enjoyment, and she gave him a smile, cupped her breasts, and lifted her hips, giving him a big hint how she felt about his question. "Bring it, but you might want to remember paybacks are coming, and I've found I like the taste of your skin." His eyes were on her mouth and she deliberately licked her lips.

CHAPTER NINE

Lonnie got the call from the hospital shortly after they got back to the bar. Stevie had dragged him through the mall. At least she'd gone into the leather shop.

While she was trying on boots, he bought a buttery soft vest for Sharon, and he added a silver arm cuff to his purchase. She would scold him for spending the money on her, but he planned to insist on a private show. He tossed in a black thong to complete the outfit and smiled while he paid for his purchases.

Stevie spent almost a grand on a jacket, boots, chaps, and gloves. The next store, he sat on the bench outside of the shop. She said he was welcome to join her in picking out panties, but she wasn't sure how John might feel about Lonnie knowing what kind of undies she owned. He was loaded down with the leather she purchased and she carried the ladies underthings.

He didn't mind carrying his woman's panties, hell, he often wore her thong on his bicep after he took it off her when they made love. This was different, and he'd be damned if he could figure out why the idea of carrying another woman's sexy underwear made him uncomfortable, but he was glad she carried her own.

At first the call made him panic. Sharon had been in a bad accident, according to the hospital, she was brought in unconscious, and he was listed as her next of kin. He wasn't the sharpest knife in the drawer, but something about the call was off.

After assuring the caller that he was on his way, he ended the call. He looked at Stevie and told her to call John.

"I'm calling the clubhouse to get someone over to where Sharon works. Unless she borrowed a car, I know for a fact she rode her putt into work this morning, we left the house together, so how else would she be in a car accident?"

Stevie didn't get to talk to John, her message went straight to his voicemail.

Lonnie was talking on the speaker feature of his phone, and texting Sharon at the same time. Her reply was immediate, and he breathed a deep sigh of relief. Leech was the one to answer the club's house phone, and once he heard what Lonnie suspected, he told them to keep the doors of the bar locked until they got there.

"We'll be there ASAP," and the line went dead.

Lonnie looked around them and then to her. "Someone wants me to leave you alone and vulnerable. We need to find a spot to hide you. Leon probably knew I'd say something to you about Harry, and chances are, he has a stash of meth or worse here somewhere that he wants back. Didn't you say he's been asking personal questions?

"Maybe he thinks if you are alone you might be talked into helping him with his sideline. The fucker gives me the creeps up my spine anytime day or night, so I'm prejudice where he's concerned. I'm going to look at the security cameras, and if it looks clear, I'll take a walk outside, I want to make sure the bastards know you aren't a sitting duck, you have backup. Do you have a key to the door that I can use?"

"Lonnie, I don't want you going out there alone, please don't make yourself a target, let's just wait for Leech and the Breed to show up, please, Sharon needs you to come home to her in one piece and with no new holes in your beautiful body. I'm afraid that you'll get shot, and I'll run outside to help you and get shot too."

He scowled at her. "That's not nice, blackmailing me like that. Believe it or not, Stevie, I am capable of self-defense, I may look like a limp wristed bastard to you, but I train and can fight with the best of the Breed." He could see she wanted to argue with him, but he was losing his temper, and now was not the time for bragging.

"Did you think John would leave your safety in an incompetent's hands?" He shook his head, "I don't think we have time for this shit, come on, let's go to the office, the door locks and I have a gun to use if I need it."

He pulled her into the small room and locked the door after them. She booted up the computer and opened the security feed to show on the monitor. Nothing was moving in the parking lots, so they relaxed in their chairs.

"Lonnie, I don't doubt your competency, I would do my best to keep you here with me regardless if you looked like Rambo.

"The truth is that I'm afraid to be here alone. After the other night, I see ninjas in every corner, and I'm so jumpy that it isn't funny. The fact you have a wife to go home to makes me worry even more for you. John's not answering his phone, so who knows where he is. Please understand, I trust you, I don't trust Leon. You are the only one who he thinks knows about him, and don't forget, Leon has a key to this place. He could come and go, so why try to get you to leave the building?"

The more he thought about it, the more convinced he was that whoever wanted him out of the building would know that he wouldn't leave Stevie unprotected, it stood to reason he would take her with him instead of letting her stay, and he voiced his thoughts to her. "We're looking at this wrong, they don't want me to leave you, they want the building empty for some reason."

Stevie looked at the monitor and gasped. "What on earth, oh God this doesn't look good."

Sure enough, there was a dark blue panel van parking in the lot by the door, and three men exited the vehicle. All of the men reached into the back of the vehicle and hefted assault rifles into their hands. Leon carried a pry bar in his empty hand.

They looked over Lonnie's truck and her Jeep, and the short man waved his gun at Leon. He shrugged his shoulders and he must have said something to appease the man, because they headed toward the door.

Stevie made an executive decision, even as Lonnie pulled a wicked looking Glock .45 semi auto from the back of his waistband.

She ran to the door, pulling it open and grabbing his hand as she went out of the safety of the room. He tried to stop her but she mouthed the words, "Trust me," he nodded and followed her through the small utility closet door. She pushed a tall rack of supplies away from the wall and gave the wall a shove. It opened into a larger room, and she pulled him in behind her, pushing the door closed. She laid a broom handle in the track, just like most people do for a sliding patio door to keep it from being muscled open.

Lonnie looked around the dimly lit space. A large bed sat in the corner, a small table with two chairs, and a desk with a computer that Stevie was booting up. One corner of the room held a small sink and cupboard. On the counter was a hotplate and under that was a dorm-sized fridge. All the comforts of home, and he'd never known it was here. "What."

She shushed him, and he wanted to laugh at the fierce look she tossed his way. She crooked her fingers to get him to come close, so he picked up the chair and sat it and himself down next to her.

She handed him an ear bud and she put the other one in her own ear while they watched the trio search the bar. The cameras were only in the common areas of the building, so there were times they could see nothing, but hearing the men stomping around was clear enough to know where they were looking. The storeroom door was slammed open with such force that it banged into the wall, and the sound of feet and searching could be heard on the other side of the closed wall/door.

Muttering and cursing could be heard as two sets of steps left the next room and Stevie let out the breath she'd been holding.

Lonnie dropped the hand with the gun pointed at the door, and set the weapon on the desk next to the keyboard. He pulled out his cell and texted Leech while Stevie went to the fridge and got two cans of soda.

She watched the monitor and saw the three men had been satisfied that they had the place to themselves and Leon began to use the crowbar on the front footboards of the small stage that she'd performed on for the past year, and it sickened her to see him pulling the little platform apart while the largest of the three men reached down and began pulling brick sized packages from the gaping hole.

The three men began hauling their find out to the van, and Stevie hoped they'd hurry up and leave. This was almost as bad as having her home broken into and the feeling of being violated made her tremble with hatred. The sexual assault hadn't bothered her much, because her assailant's excitement had barely been felt, his dick was so small that she hadn't been penetrated, and he'd ejaculated almost immediately when he touched her flesh with his. She was so filled with rage right now that she couldn't sit still. The loss of choice had frightened her at the time, and now the only thing holding her back from running out there with Lonnie's gun and shooting all three men was fear they might shoot her first, plus common sense.

Lonnie began cussing under his breath as the men finished clearing the bricks out, and they watched as Leon came back into the bar and began smashing bottles of liquor on the floor of the bar and lit a lighter, setting the tequila that was puddled on the wooden bar itself.

If they stayed in the secret room, they would die. The storage closet was directly behind the bar and the hungry fire that was spread wherever the bastard had slung the bottles.

Stevie watched Leon joyfully set his lighter to a dry bar rag, and threw it onto a table in the middle of the floor. He did the same with another rag, and soon there was nothing to see but smoke and flame. The only way they knew the bastards had left was the sound of the squealing tires from the back wall.

Lonnie looked at Stevie, and although he knew she was afraid, she looked, well, she actually looked insane at the moment, and he shook his head. She had cause enough to be a bit unbalanced.

He pulled her to stand in front of him and shook her shoulders, he could feel the tremble in her body, but they didn't have time for him to coddle her if they wanted to get out of there alive.

"Stevie, listen to me, we have to make a run for it, do you get that?" She nodded and appeared to be more focused—for now anyway—and that was all that he needed. He put his gun back in his waistband while she pulled a small white box from the computer, went to the bed, and pulled an old leather bag out from under the frame, stuffed the box inside of the thing, looked around and shook her head.

She let him take her wrist after he removed the broomstick from the doorway. "Let's do this."

How he navigated them out of the flames with little more than smoke and singed damage to their clothing was a miracle. Lonnie sat her in her Jeep and locked the doors while he ran back inside to see if he could check the electrical box near the backdoor, the panel had been open when they ran through, so he figured correctly as it turned out, that the breakers for the water pump that fed the sprinklers had been shut off. Once the double breaker was flipped back on, it took several seconds for the water to begin raining down on his head, but the bar should be salvageable.

Leech, Skids, Angus, and Preacher showed up mere seconds after he exited the building, and minutes later the fire department sirens could be heard heading their way.

The bikers left, and she still sat staring at the building. Lonnie stood outside of the truck waiting for the big red rigs to show up.

The more she thought about it, the madder she became, but the anger was a cold thing in her gut. In all probability, one of those men could have killed Harry, and revenge scenarios played through her mind. The practical side of her reasoning dismissed all but one of the plots, and she continued to make plans.

The chief of the volunteer firemen went through the building and asked her questions about the vandals, but she told them she was in the storage room with Lonnie, doing inventory when they broke in and didn't see the people who did this. She knew that if he asked, she would have to give up the security feed from the office monitor, but that only showed the parking lots and backdoor.

Luckily the chief believed the sprinkler system had drenched the computer, rendering any data useless. He was old school good ol' boy and directed most of his questions toward Lonnie, and for once in her life she was happy not to be considered a capable woman.

She walked inside the building with the chief and Lonnie, and couldn't believe the level of destruction done in such a short span of time. What the fire hadn't ruined, the water did. She walked into the office and picked up the bags with her new purchases inside, and took them to her Jeep.

Lonnie was busy with the chief and another man when she walked up and told the men that she was not feeling well. "I think I just need to go home and lie down for a little while, if you don't need me for anything else?"

The old man nodded and patted her on the shoulder in understanding. "Naw, that's fine, darlin', you ladies aren't used to stuff like this happenin' I guess it's the kind of thing that happens mostly when a man least expects it, but it shouldn't happen to a woman business owner. Might want to think about some other business to go into. Mary Jane Old's is thinking of retiring, and her boutique does a good business. You can tell her I told you to give her a call."

Lonnie was watching her with narrowed eyes and started toward her, but the chief had already dismissed her from his mind and took his arm to have him show the old man where they'd been when the fire started.

Stevie felt bad about trapping her bodyguard like this, but she needed some alone time, and she didn't need a babysitter where she was going. She nodded at him in understanding, and walked out of the building.

Thankfully the Jeep started, and the fire truck wasn't blocking her from leaving the property. She headed to the only secluded spot that she could think of to clean up and get ready. John wasn't home when she got there and she didn't have a key, but she did have a credit card and slid it between the door and the jam to release the locks. It worked, and she was shocked that it worked, but walked inside with her purchases anyway.

She looked longingly at that tub again, but couldn't take the time. Hopefully he wouldn't hold a grudge for her defection, but this one was hers. She had a heritage that she'd left behind the day her parents walked through the prison doors. It was time to reintroduce herself to the world as who she really was.

By the time she walked out of the sanctuary deep in the woods, no one would recognize the biker chick from her former hippie chick look. Her hair was pulled back in a leather wrap, her jacket was hanging by two fingers over her shoulder, the skintight jeans and buckle boots made her appear taller, and the tank under the partially snapped vest completed her outfit. She carried the leather bag in her empty hand, and got in the Jeep.

It was more than time to confront Stevie Ray James, daughter of Rolf and June Bug James. Two of the most infamous outlaw bikers in the state of

Alabama. The Feds had only been able to pin one count each of Drug trafficking and the RICO charges had been dropped on appeal due to lack of evidence. Unless some ultra-smart Fed had dug up more charges, her parents should have walked into the sun over a year ago.

When Harry slipped her out of that foster home, it had been a blessing. The people weren't bad, but they did tend to lecture her on being churchy and they tried to get her to talk about her parents. Harry told her afterwards the family was kin to the federal prosecutor who was shoveling every charge he could think of to keep Rolf and June Bug incarcerated for as many years as possible.

She owed Harry her life, and her parents were about to see what had become of their little Stevie.

CHAPTER TEN

John was searching the area around Egypt, Arkansas, when he checked his phone to see if he had enough tower service to make a call to Stevie and Lonnie. He was planning to find a place to bed down for the night, and resume his search for Candle. That fuck was earning himself some extra pain before he met his mentor, the devil.

There were eighteen messages waiting for him to hear, and from Stevie's first call to the last call from a very pissed off Lonnie, he grew more concerned. She'd given Lonnie the slip, and done it deliberately.

There were two text messages from Stevie, and he breathed a sigh of relief that she was safe. The last text just pissed him off.

Sorry, I need to do this, tired of being a victim. That's not who I am. I'll be in touch to explain next week.

That was it, her phone went directly to voice, and she didn't return his texts either.

His brain was not going to allow him to sleep, and he had a few hours before he would need to find a place to camp, so he turned the bike toward the Swamp Rats nesting ground. Pappy D swore he couldn't find Candle to talk to him, and John knew the old man was lying through the few teeth that were left in his mouth.

The way John figured it was that if he busted up enough of the fucks, they would turn on their comrade. He was done being nice about this shitass. It was time to do some serious damage, there was too much to deal with at home right now, and his woman was out joyriding and being too damn reckless with her life.

When he got a hold on her ass, she was gonna feel it.

Once he got near Murky Carl's Bayou Gator farm, he almost busted a nut trying to find a dry enough spot to set the kickstand securely to keep the scoot from falling over. He finally saw a tree root that was mostly buried in the muddy dirt, and set the kickstand. Damn, he was going to have to get back into working out, pushing his favorite heavy assed bitch around in the mud was work.

He slid twice in the mud going through the trees running down the path instead of walking on the path itself, he wasn't familiar with the property, and didn't want to be target practice for some Rat.

When he saw the shack on the water's edge, he wondered what was going on inside. He could hear screams coming from inside the building, and circled the perimeter in an effort to make sure there were no guards lying in wait.

There was shouting and the sidewall of the shanty shook as if it was considering giving way beneath the pressure of a body being thrown against the rotting wood. The smell of Meth cooking was intense, but it was mingled with the scent of rotting vegetation and swamp, so he could understand why they chose this place to cook the shit.

*****

Tonda was worried sick about Donnie Lee. He was an asshole with a taste for sadism, but she liked most of what he liked, so she couldn't bitch too much about his methods. She still wondered how they'd captured him. Donnie was a fighter, a dirty fighter at that. Being the son of ol' Pappy D didn't give him special treatment, if anything he was picked on more often and always having to prove he was worthy of the name Dean.

She was the product of Lila Bennett who was a waitress at the diner in town and some passing soldier boy named Curtis that came out of the hills to join in Uncle Sam's Army. Tonda was the result of his going away party. Lila was wandering around town nowadays talking to trees and picking up beer cans to recycle for a few extra dollars each month.

Tonda had given up going into town and bringing her to live in the small travel trailer that sat on blocks behind the clubhouse. The woman would stay for a day or two and disappear. She wasn't aware that Tonda was her daughter, she wasn't aware of much of anything but the voices in her head. The cops picked her up and let her sleep in the jail on cold nights, and Tonda made sure the woman had a decent pair of shoes on her feet and sweaters and coats to keep her warm. The soup kitchen knew Lila by name and always had a meal for her when she came in.

Donnie had befriended Tonda when he stopped some older boys from their intent to rape her in the alley behind the Laundromat in town one day when she was walking home from school. She'd worshipped him from that day on. If Donnie asked

111

her to sell herself on a corner in the worst part of Little Rock, she wouldn't like it, but she would do it, because he asked her to. She gave him her virginity, in every hole, and he didn't stay faithful, but he did give her a place to live and a job of sorts. Her hopes of setting up house with him had long ago been shattered, especially when he encouraged other men to fuck her like the whore she was. He was a cold hearted fucker, but she loved him, and she was disgusted that old fucker Pappy D refused to turn Candle over to the bastard who had Donnie.

Candle was a troublemaker who liked to hurt anyone smaller than he was, and given the fact he was almost six foot tall meant that there were several people around that qualified as smaller, most of them were women. He thieved and liked to play with his hunting knife while taunting his sex partners.

When she came up with her plan, it sounded better than it actually played out. She had her belongings in the backseat of the car before she left to get close to Candle and zap his ass with the Taser she stole from one of the bikers she fucked the day before.

She'd wished she'd told Allan if he didn't hear from her to come and rescue her. Her plan was going well until Candle decided he needed a little fear from her to give him a hard-on. He backhanded her and it was on. He got the fear he wanted, and the screams, and the drops of blood from the prick of his knife poking at her skin. Her hands were roped together behind her and she was out of options but the need to live long enough to get loose and find her purse where she hid the Taser.

She didn't see what happened next. Candle was lifted from her body, and she heard the crash of his body as it was slammed into the table and chairs. She crawled to the wall and felt the knife drop on the floor as she inched away from the fight behind her. It took every bit of strength she could muster to push herself up enough for the wall to hold her as she leaned on it. She was praying for the Lord to help her survive long enough to help set Donnie free.

The sounds of grunting and fists hitting flesh made her look at the two combatants, and she gasped. This had to be the man who was hunting for Candle. They said he was a big man, with dark hair, and had tats. They hadn't said that the man was so well built or that he carried himself like a warrior.

The raw scream coming from Candle's bloody lips took her attention from the stranger's thick tattooed arms in time to see him proceed to beat the sadistic bastard's face into a red mush. She looked away when the big hands grabbed Candle's head and gave it a solid twist. It was the first time Tonda had seen anyone killed, but after seeing the disgust on the victor's face, she got the impression he was disappointed Candle hadn't put up a better fight.

She tried to stay silent, hoping he wouldn't notice her sitting there, but he looked at her before Candle's body collapsed onto the floor. She cringed, but there was nowhere for her to hide, and she resigned herself to dying because she was witness to the death of a man who wasted space and the air he breathed.

"Mr., I," she had to swallow back her fear before trying to speak to him again, "I was gonna bring him to you but he surprised me before I could catch him off guard. You saved my life, and I thank you, but I just wanted to get you to let Donnie Lee go. This didn't go like I planned." She broke down and cried as the big man came toward her.

John knew the woman was afraid, she should be. From what he'd seen when he walked into the room, she was lucky the fucker hadn't killed her. He looked around the room and spied a case of bottled water on an old dry sink. He went to the spot and took two bottles from the dirty plastic wrapping. He kept his movements slow as he crouched down near where she was sitting. He looked at her bloody wrists that were still wrapped with yellow nylon rope, and pulled his knife from his boot to cut the rope while she tried to pull away from him.

The blade slid through the nylon with ease, and her hands dropped down hard. As he reached for one of the water bottles and unscrewed the cap, he began talking in a low tone to her.

"Here you go, I think you could probably use something to wet your whistle." He held the bottle to her lips and tilted it slightly so she could drink without drenching herself. After a few swallows, he sat the bottle next to her hip and moved back a bit to give her some space. At least she wasn't hysterical. If he heard her right, she almost lost her own life in an attempt to ruin her own and save her worthless man. Did she even know that by being here and attempting what she'd planned, would get her shunned by the Swamp Rats?

"Did I hear you right? You were the only one of your pack that had the guts to do the right thing? Tell me, would you have killed him if necessary to get Donnie back?"

She didn't know how to answer him, "Mr., we all seen what shape you've been sending the brothers back in. Willy boy wasn't the sharpest tool in the shed to begin with, now his momma says he started lickin' his lips all the time, an' she says between the way he already had a stutter, the lip lickin' is even more brain damage. The clubhouse is beginning to look like the medical clinic."

She looked over to Candle's body still lying where it'd dropped. "I had to do somethin', nobody else would lift a finger to help him, Donnie Lee I mean. They'd let you kill him before they would turn this piece of shit over, it ain't right. That's all, it just ain't right."

She looked up when the big man pulled his t-shit off and handed it to her. The material was still warm as she fumbled her arms inside and pulled her head through the neck. The feeling was returning to her hands and Lord they stung. "Thank you."

"Mr.? What happens now?" He had a bottle of water to his lips and she could see him swallow as he drained the plastic container within a minute or so. "I, are you satisfied now, I mean enough to let Donnie come home?"

John looked at the woman, still sitting where she'd crawled to against the wall. She was a mess, there was no two ways about it, and he couldn't let her stay alone to face the shit when the Rats figured out she had been here tonight. He wondered what Baron would have to say about taking on a woman with the reputation for breaking the code, but at least he could give her a place to stay until she decided what to do or where she would go if she didn't stay with the Breed.

He nodded his head and walked over to help her up off the planked floor. "Are you in any shape to drive?" She licked her lips and nodded, so he didn't bother to try to coddle her. She needed to get some miles put between her and the Swamp Kings.

"Is that your car out there with the backseat filled with boxes and trash bags?"

Tonda shook her head no. "The car belongs to the club, I was just gonna use it to transport Candle and exchange him for Donnie, that way he'd have a way to make it home."

He reached into his front pocket and pulled out a small wad of money. She shook her head when he tried to hand her a hundred dollar bill, so he peeled off a couple of twenties and she hesitated a few seconds before taking it. "I'm only taking this 'cause I think the car's gonna need gas."

He shrugged his shoulders, "Up to you what you spend it on, you look like you could use a meal, but wearing my shirt isn't gonna get you into any fast food place that I know of. When you get to the club, look me up or talk to Baron, he'll know what you're there for, I have something I need to take care of so I might not be there."

He handed her the dead man's wallet and she hesitated before taking it from his hands. She opened the wide leather and took the few bills that had been left. She glanced at her rescuer, and looked to every corner of the run down shack. She smiled, knowing what she was going to do. The Swamp Kings would never know what happened, she would be long gone, and so would the Breed.

She walked over to the propane burner and turned it on, once it lit she glanced behind her and smiled at the man that was shaking his head no. She began to laugh, and told him, "Mr., you did me a favor and I'm going to do this part of the world a big favor too. I know I won't be back here again so let's just call this payback." She turned the next burner on and stood back far enough to watch the flames. Then walked toward where John stood in the open doorway. "You might want to get a move on it, I got the oven on and the pilot light off, It's gonna blow this place to hell, and take that poison shit with it."

She grinned at him through her bloody split lips, lifted her hand to wave to him and did her best to run for the car.

John took a page from the white trash handbook and ran as fast as he could through the trees to get back to his scoot. His arms were tired and his thighs felt like rubber, but he got the Harley out of the trees in record time and he left the track at the same time the cabin blew. From the sound of the explosion, they must have had a large operation going there, but right now he was in no mood to be seen in the area. Hurting men was one thing, but

117

destroying a money making operation was entirely a different thing.

He was going to have to put some miles between him and Arkansas tonight, or the Swamp Kings would have recourse. His hunt was over.

He was passing the state line when he saw the Olds getting on the highway behind him a half a mile or so back, and figured the woman must have stopped for fuel and was heading for the clubhouse. He would be at his house when she arrived, but he had to clean up before he showed up at the club. It was gonna take a hell of a lot of soap to wash the stink of the swamp from his body and clothes.

The first thing he did when he parked the bike was to hose as much mud and road film off it as he could. He left it in the carport and went inside to shower.

As the hot water sluiced down his chest, he thought of Stevie and his dick got hard. He was going to enjoy baring her ass and turning it red as a beet. He made a mental note to stop at the toy store Baron and Gunner owned up by the highway, and pick up a few things she might like.

Washing his hard prick led to the need to drain the damn thing and he groaned, imagining it was her mouth surrounding his flesh as he ran his dick through his fingers, spewing his cum through the soapy palm of his hand.

His cell was ringing as he stepped from the steamy bathroom, and listened to Hightits telling him to get his ass over there pronto.

The message was short and to the point. "Baron just left to meet you at the club, and that woman you called about earlier is here."

*****

She drove most of the night to get here without attracting the cops, and was thankful that she made it before her right eye swelled shut like the left one had done less than an hour ago. The handsome young men at the gate had taken one look at her and waved her through even as he began punching numbers into a cell phone.

She had to wait in her car for another half an hour until another man rode his bike into the space next to her car. He looked at her and the backseat, and waited for her to speak.

"Mr. uh, the big guy with the dark hair and, I forgot to ask his name like a dummy, well he said to come here and look him up or a guy name of Baron."

The handsome smiling man opened her car door. She knew he was looking at her wrists, and tried to bring them down to her sides.

He saw her bare legs and the marks on her wrists where the rope had cut in, but didn't say anything. His hand slowly reached for hers, and she reluctantly gave it to him, allowing herself to be helped from the vehicle.

"Do you want to bring in a change of clothes, we have a room that you can take a shower and change into something warmer if you like. No one will disturb you and there's a lock on the door if you want to use it."

He kept staring at her and when she realized he was waiting for her to introduce herself, she nodded as well as her neck would allow and told him. "I'm pleased to meet you. I'm Tonda."

"Well, Tonda, they call me Leech, let's see if we can get you comfortable, and as soon as John gets here and sorts this all out, we can offer you some refreshment and some sort of breakfast while you wait."

So now she was still in the room they'd been allowing her to use, and was afraid they might have forgotten her. That good looking bastard had told her they'd come get her once John got there, but it seemed to have been hours since he'd left her. She was startled when the knock on the door finally sounded, and called for the person to come in.

The rumors were fact. He was a big mother. Dark hair with tats running down his arms from neck to wrists, she knew for a fact those tats didn't stop at his shoulders. They decorated his back and part of his chest too. She could see why Mel kept sayin' that he and Willie didn't have a hope in hell of taking this guy down. There was something attractive about him, but she was too fuckin' tired to worry about that now.

"I've been waitin' for long enough, Mr. Unless you already killed him, but I would know, I think, if he was dead. I'm tired, and I need to see Donnie this last time before he goes home. Mr., I'm begging you for this one favor, and we'll be outta your way."

The woman was beaten to hell and bruised until both of her eyes were almost swollen completely shut, but she had come for her man. She knew no club would allow a rat to stay within the group, but she'd braved shunning to save the Swamp Rat.

Leech told him it looked like she had everything she owned in the backseat of her car, and when John found Candle at the shack, he saw the garbage bags and cardboard boxes for himself. He made a decision and nodded at Leech who was right behind him.

Leech and Burger would move her shit out of the vehicle to the room here, and she could have time to heal or decide to stay. The choice would be hers, the woman had heart, and she had courage. Both were qualities the men admired. Donnie Lee Dean was a dumb bastard who had no idea what he would be throwing away when he left here without her.

"You did the right thing, I know it probably doesn't seem like it, but looking at you right now, you must know that you saved more women from that fucker. You're brave, and if that little fucker doesn't appreciate you, then it's his loss. This room is yours for as long as you need it, and from what I can see, it's gonna take at least a week before you will be able to see again, so you're in a good place to rest and heal."

"I'll bring the Swamp Rat to you, he can take your car back to where he came from, and we'll call it even. You don't have to go back and catch a bunch of shit."

He turned and left the room.

Donnie Lee was lying on his back thinking about home. When he became the prez, he was gonna make the Swamp Kings into a group that was respected by other bikers. He knew the Breed were some evil mothers, but they hadn't touched him. The other two men still screamed in the middle of the night, but even their cries had slowed down to once or twice a night.

The door opened and that cold fucker walked into his cell. The dark-haired son-of-a-bitch was with him.

It was the big fucker who reached down and grabbed him by the front of his shirt, pulled him to his feet, and slammed him against the wall. It didn't hurt much, the only damage he felt was done to his pride, but Leech grabbed his ankles and snapped the shackles on. The leash was removed, but they still hadn't said anything, and that worried him a bit. Had they gotten tired of waiting? Was it his turn to suffer like his brothers in the other cells? A bag was placed over his head, and he tried to struggle, but the two men let him wear himself out before one of them pulled him down a long hallway and up some stairs.

He was so confused that nothing made sense. He had been led outside, and then inside another building, until his captor stopped. The hood was taken from his head, and the shackles released from his legs. The last thing to be removed was the cuffs, but no one made a move to release his hands.

John enjoyed the fear he saw on the younger man's face, but he worried about the girl in the room in front of them.

"You are one lucky son-of-a-bitch, someone is about to learn what an ungrateful fuck Pappy D raised, but you don't deserve loyalty and the courage I saw today. I doubt if she'll think you're worth the sacrifice when you come out of the room."

The door was opened, and he was shoved into the room. The door shut behind him, and before he could wonder what the fucker was talking about, he saw Tonda sitting on a small bed in the corner of the room. He had to look closer to be sure it was her. Seeing the way she'd been beat on enraged him.

"Who the fuck did that?" She whimpered and made a sobbing noise, before moving as if she was in pain to stand next to the bed. She held out her hand and he knew, she was here for more than just to say hello. "What did you do, Tonda? Tell me you didn't find a way to bring Candle here, tell me you didn't betray the Kings."

She was crying and trying to talk. Nothing came out of her throat, so she swallowed again. "Candle did this to me, and I was worried about you. Donnie Lee, I had to try to help you, don't you see that? They said the Breed snatched you right off the side of the road. With all of the damage this guy did to the other men, I worried that he'd kill you. I know how bad your temper can get."

She sat back down when Donnie didn't approach her, she took a deep breath and told him of her plan. "Things didn't go like I planned, he was so fucked up on that poison shit, he went wild on me. If someone hadn't helped me, I'd be dead by now, and he'd be feedin' my ass to those gators."

She hung her head, tired of talking, just bone weary of the whole damn subject. "Donnie Lee, I've loved you since you picked me up off the ground when I was in high school. I know I was always a charity case for you. After school, I was just another whore you brought to the club to play your games with."

She leaned back against the wall behind her. Talked out. She knew he'd be like this when she planned to abduct Candle and exchange him for Donnie. Somewhere in the back of her mind, yeah, buried deep, but somewhere, she pictured them being together forever. It was what kept her bending over and allowing herself to be used by anyone who wanted her, Donnie wanted her to and so she did.

He almost shit his pants when he saw her sitting on that bed, and he knew then and there she was the reason he was free from his cell. She had to know she couldn't go back to the group with him, and damned her, it wasn't her place to be rescuing him. He could understand why she did it, she was a woman and a split tail didn't live by the biker code like men of honor did.

"Do you think I'm gonna thank you for this? You broke the rules, and you got your ass handed to you. There's a reason we men don't allow no women in the group, they got no morals or loyalty. Did you think I would take you back and pretend that you aren't a damn snake? You say you love me, well this ain't the way to prove it, and now you damn sure won't get a second chance you stupid whore."

He walked up to her and looked down at the pathetic mess Candle had turned her into. "I sure hope you think losing everything we gave you was worth it."

Her head came up and she looked at him through the slits of her eyes. "Was it worth it? I thought your life was worth any sacrifice." Her head was too heavy to hold up any longer, and she allowed it to dip back down, feeling the tears drop onto her hands. "Just go, Donnie Lee. Go home and forget about me. You'll find some other whore to play with soon enough. Just go please, just take the car, and leave."

Donnie went to the door and was surprised to find it opened when he turned the knob. He looked back at Tonda and shook his head, hating to leave her here, but knowing he couldn't take her home with him. She betrayed him and every member of the Kings, now she had to live with the consequences, just as he had to live with knowing she wouldn't be coming back and why.

CHAPTER ELEVEN

Stevie's Roots

Thor's Legion was one of the most feared MC groups in the country. They were blatant, brash, and outright outrageous. Citizens in the community loved it there, the town was slowly getting bigger, but the population was gaining numbers almost daily. The Legion established its influence long ago, and the last burglary was over ten years old. No one with a brain in their head came into Wescott, Alabama, with breaking the law on their agenda. It would be a revelation for outsiders to know that the hundred or so bikers that lived in the small township actually kept the riff raff out. The Legion didn't piss in their own backyard, and weren't about to allow anyone else to take a shit in it.

That's not to say they didn't raise a little hell away from home. If other communities couldn't keep their own places protected, it wasn't the Legion's place to moralize for them. Life as a Thor's Legion MC member put them as elite in the few 1% groups, and they enjoyed the benefits.

There were smaller chapters scattered throughout the Southern states, and a few scattered throughout the mid-west, Wescott was the mother chapter.

At times, the Feds decided to target them to investigate. To be fair, there were times the Feds would ask a favor or two in exchange for information or a less than legal activity that needed doing, but the chicken shits were too bound by politics to take care of it themselves. The special favor was never mentioned again, but money, goods, or charges against one or more of the Legion were dropped for lack of evidence.

Such was the case of Rolf and June Bug James. They'd been sentenced to seven years each, but served only three of those years, and instead of parole, they got community service. Unfortunately, by the time anyone had thought about the couple's children being left to fend for themselves, the state had snagged Stevie, and Harry disappeared off the radar.

It was a bitter crack in the family structure of the chapter, and June Bug hadn't given up finding her kids. Something bad had to have happened for Harry not to come back to the club, and the county had no explanation for Stevie's disappearance. The foster family had left the state under a cloud of suspicion, especially given the evidence of a familial relationship with a top Federal investigator who had an overt hard-on for arresting bikers, who worked in the gangs division.

Rolf James distained the notions that some people chose to believe. The rumors were just that and he had no problem laughing at the more outrageous of the bunch. He was sitting at the end of the bar listening to the three punks behind him at the table in the corner discussing him. June Bug was working the beer flippers drawing buckets and drafts for the thirsty patrons. He laughed out loud upon hearing one of the few truthful exploits he was actually guilty of doing, and June turned to see what amused him. He indicated the table behind him with his thumb, and she shook her head at him with a smile.

"Man, did you ever see the video of the big motherfucker tossing that Fed bastard through a plate glass window? He took six of those sons-a-bitches on and knocked them all on their asses, sent them to the hospital, and one dumbass stumbled over his buddy and landed on a chair leg, bloody fuckin mess.

"Ol' Rolf, there he stood in the middle of the room like a berserker or some shit. They shot him three times, blood was drippin' all over the fuckin' place and there he was, roaring like a goddamned grizzly with that Fed hanging over his head before he threw him. Fuckin' impressive."

Another voice chimed in and Rolf stopped laughing.

"They grabbed his daughter and sent her inside to talk him down. She got through to him by tossing a pitcher of beer over his head. By the way, I don't recommend anyone else try that on him, he'd probably hurt you bad."

The shouted enthusiastic approval made Rolf smile, but the last voice was a female's voice who teased the back of his mind. His beer was halfway to his lips when it hit him. The beer glass bounced on the bar as his attention turned toward the spot he heard the voice coming from.

There, her back was facing him, and he could see her hair was still worn long. The blond strands at the end of the hair wrap were unmistakable in color. He walked up behind her within touching distance and continued the story while the three young tuffs watched open-mouthed when the girl turned around crying, "Daddy," while the huge man grabbed her and pulled her tight into his arms, tears ran down his bearded cheeks unashamedly.

"That girl was the only thing that saved those cum stains from the slab, they never should have threatened my family."

The ear splitting scream and breaking glass broke the sudden silence caused by the open display of emotion from the arguably meanest fucker in the group. June Bug ran up to the two and was pulled into their embrace.

Clapping and cheers began from the table back by the jukebox, and seemed to roll over the room as they stood together in the middle of the aisle.

The younger people didn't know what they were witnessing, but the elders did, and it was cause for celebration. History was again being made by the James family. After all, how many times did the presumed dead rise and walk through your door?

Stevie Ray James was home.

The small family separated when Jonah and Bull came in the front door and started yelling for a beer. Jonah didn't have time to duck the pitcher of beer that came sailing through the air toward him, hitting him squarely upside his head.

Rolf hadn't even thought about it, when the fucker came in like that and disrupted the moment with Stevie, he'd reached down on the table closest to him and heaved the pitcher before he even realized he'd done it.

"You got your fuckin' beer, asswipe, shut up and sit ya ass down or leave the way you came in."

Stevie was laughing through her tears, and June Bug held tight to his arm to keep him from further disturbing their reunion with their daughter. He shook his head and shrugged. He apologized to no one, that fuck got what he deserved.

"You got some talkin' to do, girlie, but it can wait for now." He looked at June Bug through his own watery eyes, "Ain't that right, momma?"

For the first time in years, the woman who held his heart in the palm of her hand smiled at the affectionate term "momma". When they'd gotten out from behind bars, and found that their children were gone, and that Stevie had disappeared from the "secure" foster home. A light in her eyes dimmed, she asked him not to call her that again until they found the kids.

"I love you to death, but it's like a needle sticking in my gut every time I hear that word."

She followed her parents' home from the tavern that they'd taken over when they were released from the "darkness" as her dad called prison. Her mother hadn't said much, but she had kept touching her, and Stevie was beginning to understand how much her parents had missed her and Harry. When her dad asked about Harry, and she shook her head, her huge tough father's shoulders had slumped, and she saw desolation on his face for maybe a second. His next expression was narrow-eyed determination.

"When we get home, I want to know." She'd nodded, and he nodded. It was one of those Biker things she guessed. They could say complete sentences with just a nod of the head to one another.

Her parents had been young when her mom got pregnant with Harry, at fifteen years old, she watched sixteen-year-old Rolf allow her father to beat the shit out of him for knocking his little girl up before she graduated from high school. The only thing that had saved her from her father's belt had been the fact she waited until she was four months along in her pregnancy to tell anyone, and he was afraid he would hurt the baby.

They were still in their mid-forties, and looked great. Stevie remembered how she would come home from school bringing a friend with her, and walk in on her parents lying on the living room floor, wrestling around with her dad tickling her mom on her neck with his prickly beard. She always rolled her eyes and told them they had a room for that, but her father told her, "The whole fuckin' house is ours, anybody that gets a tickle in their ass seeing us playin' around doesn't deserve to be in our home anyway. Fuck 'em."

Those memories had lingered with her over the years, and seeing them today brought home to her how much she'd missed them. She wished Harry was there too, but if he was alive, she had no idea where to look for him, and he wouldn't leave her alone and unprotected voluntarily. She felt like a fraud coming here, they thought she was here because she just found out they were out of jail. Harry had always told her they couldn't go back, that if they went back to the club, their parents would suffer, and so they stayed away. She hoped that Harry was wrong, because if she was going to avenge her brother and the damage to the bar, she would need help.

John might have helped her if she'd asked, but she wanted to prove that she was strong, she had to do this for her. John was a Neanderthal and would want to take over the task she'd set for herself, but it wasn't his business, and she was the one that had to live with herself after the fact. He acted like she was his, but a couple of fucks didn't make it so. Aside from the fact that she needed to deal with her parents, she was planning to kill a man to avenge her brother, and she needed to know what Harry meant by hurting her parents if they came back. None of it made sense, but hopefully they'd get it sorted out.

The house was a nice three bedroom, two bath, with an attached two car garage brick ranch, and it sat right in the center of the block.

Her parents parked the Road King in the garage, and she had to smile about the bike. Years ago her father wouldn't have been caught dead on such a fancy ride. He was old school with his preference of ride. It was the main reason June Bug got her own ride, she complained about the bitch pad numbing her lady parts.

When Stevie was thirteen she got her own scoot, but didn't get a license until after she and Harry had been on the road for a few years. It was something she planned to remedy soon, she needed her own bike. No matter where she ended up, or who she ended up with, she wanted her own transportation.

Riding with John on the bagger hadn't been a hardship, but his daily ride, she could sympathize with her mother. Damn, she had to quit thinking about him like this. He was bossy, and he was so testosterone driven that he reminded her of someone, *Oh fuckin' no*. She realized who he reminded her of.

The man striding out of the garage, coming toward her to carry her bag, her father was an older, hairier, version of the same cut of man as John was. She didn't have daddy issues, no one had ever measured up to the man her father was, until John. Personality wise they were polar opposites, where Rolf James was large and in charge, John Handy was quiet and reasonable, as long as you did it his way. *Fuck, just fuck.* It was a good thing that she wasn't in love with John yet, she would look around for a more compatible man.

Her door opened and her father looked at her with concern. "You okay, baby? You've been sitting her staring at the house for a bit, you ain't thinking about disappearing again, are you?"

She shook her head. "No, I was just thinking, sorry, I seem to be having a hard time realizing that you and Mom are here and… Oh, Daddy, you have no idea how much I've missed the two of you."

She slid out of the driver's seat, and grabbed him by the arm, holding onto him while he opened the back flap and pulled the old leather carpetbag from the space. He hefted the familiar bag and stared at it for a few seconds before giving her another of those concerned looks. "You sure Harry is dead?"

"No, Daddy, I'm not sure of anything right now, all I know is that when things got too much for me,

I made it my business to try to find you and Mom. I need help to sort it out, and who else would understand what is happening if not the three of us, I have more questions than answers."

They walked into the house and June Bug pounced on her baby girl. She held onto Stevie, and there was no question whether she had been missed. "Baby, I prayed, I prayed so hard to find you. We've hired people to track you and Harry but nothing came of it. Now you're here, just walked in the door like I haven't been worried sick wondering if you are in a safe place and happy. You have no idea how happy I am right now. Come on, I'll show you to your room. Oh, baby, I am so damn happy right now."

Stevie let herself be drawn down the hallway. Her mother needed to talk to her, and truthfully, she wanted to hear her mother's voice.

CHAPTER TWELVE

They sat on the edge of the narrow twin bed and June Bug held Stevie to her shoulder, patting her arm and begging for forgiveness for abandoning her and Harry.

"Baby, that piece of shit lawyer told us we'd get probation or I would have refused to take the fall for that shit. We were lucky to get the sentence down after the fact. We were supposed to be home that night. Everyone was surprised when they took us into the prison that same day."

It was Stevie's turn to hold her mother, "Momma, I know what happened, Harry came and got me, he snuck into the bedroom window and we left that night. I was only there a couple of weeks.

"The foster home was just a married couple, who was either indebted to the Fed, or related to the man they called Pascal. They were really not happy that I told them I didn't know anything about the club, or what you and Daddy did when you weren't home.

"Harry did a good job of keeping us safe and fed, you'd be proud of him. One of the club brother's told him to get away from the club and if we ever showed back up that you and Daddy would be in worse trouble than what you already were. I swear we talked about coming back, but Harry was afraid to cause you anymore hurt. I have so much to tell you about Harry and me, but right now I am really tired. I've been driving since yesterday afternoon. Do you think I could sleep for a couple of hours?"

Her mother became all hustle and nodded her head, "Oh, sweetheart, of course. You go ahead and have a sleep. The bathroom's right across the hall." She couldn't help herself, she caught Stevie in a breath stealing embrace. "You have no idea how happy I am that you're back. Dream big, honey."

Stevie's bag sat just inside the door, so she went over to it and hefted the thing onto the bed. She pulled out the extra clothes she'd brought with her and picked out a pair of shorts and a t-shirt to sleep in. She walked across the hall to the bathroom and took a quick shower before going back to her room and falling into the bed. She was asleep within minutes of her head touching the pillow.

June Bug looked in on her at eleven, but she was still out. She went back to the big bed she shared with Rolf.

His big body was lying under the covers with one arm propped behind his shaggy head. She almost ran to the bed and jumped on top of the only man she'd ever loved. She bounced, giggling and hugged his wide chest. She sat up and put his hands on his head. "Our baby is home. Oh, Rolf, our baby is here where she belongs, and my heart is so full right now, you have no idea."

Her eyes dimmed a little, but she kept the smile on her face, and he knew it was for his sake. There was still one missing, and if he wasn't coming home, well, they'd deal with it when Stevie woke up in the morning. Tonight they would have a small celebration.

After June fell asleep on his chest, he found he couldn't sleep. He tenderly rolled her onto her side of the bed, and moved the covers from where he'd lain and covered her sexy body. He shook his head at his sappy thoughts, but he would kill, lie, cheat, whatever it took to make her smile.

He went back down the hallway he'd just gone through an hour and a half ago. He came out of the bathroom in the hallway and almost collided with Stevie. He grabbed her arms to stop her from bouncing off his big body and she squeaked, and then to his surprise she giggled. He picked her up and kept walking toward the kitchen.

Just before he sat her in the chair, he kissed her cheek and gave her an extra squish. He grabbed a beer from the fridge, and offered it to her, she smiled and thanked him. The sub sandwich he tossed on the table was yesterday's leftovers, but he figured it was still edible, so he pulled a knife from the block, sat down and unwrapped the multi meat, light on the garden filled bun. He raised an eyebrow in her direction and she grinned and held her hand palm out, wiggling her fingers in a gimme gesture.

"Baby girl, it's damn good to have you home. Your momma's been worried sick over you." He looked at the half sandwich in his hand and looked back to her. "Truth, I've been just as bad as she is. I heard her telling you what happened, so you know I took care of that fuck lawyer as soon as I found out he'd double crossed us with that cocksucker Pascal. By then the damage was done." He picked up the sandwich again and stared at it, the thing was dropped and he sat back in his chair.

"Stevie, I love you, and don't you ever fuckin' think you are not enough for me. I held you the

137

minute you were born and you took a nice thick slice of my heart too. Thing is, I ain't gonna sleep until you tell me what happened to Harry. I know it's not good, but if he's not coming back, well I need to know that too."

She nodded her head, "Yeah, well it is a confusing thing, so let me get what I have, and you can tell me if he's dead, or just gone, because I have doubts, but it might be wishful thinking on my part." As she walked past him to retrieve the leather bag, she asked if they had a computer. He nodded and pointed to the living room, so she kept walking.

When she came out of the bedroom, her father had a brand new laptop in his hands that he had just taken from the box. She grinned. There was wrapping paper scattered around the floor, and she had to ask. "Who's the present for? It's not my birthday."

"Still a smart ass aren't you? It is a present for your mother, she wore the keys off the old one searching websites and message boards. We never gave up hope, baby girl, not for a day, not for a damn minute. Now since you're so fuckin' smart, you need to plug this thing in."

She sat the bag down on the counter and dug inside for the two files she had of information about Harry's accident, and the police report and pictures. "Here you go, this will keep you busy while I do your light work here." She handed them over and found the cord and plugged it into the receptacle while she looked for the old computer router.

She had the laptop up and running with her external hard drive plugged into the USB port. She looked up and saw the way her father traced the picture of the burnt bike. He had tears trailing down his cheeks like she had the first time she'd seen the photos.

She went behind him and rubbed his shoulders, and leaned down next to his ear. "Look at the bike, does it look like a wrecked bike? Does it look like it went over a gorge? The tags are legit, they belonged to Harry's bike, but there isn't a mark on the scoot. The tank is in one piece and not even dinged up, and look at the forks, I'm no expert, but it is haunting me. The body they found was burned beyond any form of identification, and I never saw the body, they gave me no choice but to accept what they told me.

"Now, I told you about the bar, right? This guy is a real asshole, and maybe you can tell me what I'm not seeing here. The footage is from the past week."

She went to the bathroom and when she came back out, her father was going through the bag on the counter.

"What are you looking for? All you had to do was ask, I'm not sneaking drugs in here you know."

He barely glanced her way as he removed everything in the bag. Including the .45 semi auto. He looked at her with a raised eyebrow. She shrugged and he began tearing the lining out of the bag. The material pulled loose effortlessly beneath his tugs, and the thin slat of wood from the bottom of the bag came out and Rolf slumped back onto the counter as he pulled a small notepad from the space.

So this was why Harry told her to grab the bag if she could in case of an emergency. She thought he wanted it saved because it was all he had left of the old life.

He was smiling at first, as he read what the notepad contained, his demeanor changed, and he began cussing very low. By the time he was clutching the note in his hand, he was heading to the bedroom.

Stevie watched the big man stride from the room and she followed. Her father hadn't shut the door, he was reaching into the closet and came out with two wooden boxes. She had an idea what was in those boxes, but was not quite prepared to see the wicked looking knife clutched in his big fist. There was a rounded guard where four of his fingers slid through to clutch in his fist. The other box contained a set of handguns. One was shoved into the back of his beltline and the other he carried in his free hand. He disappeared from her sight for a few minutes and she heard whispers, so rather than eavesdrop, she ran to her room and got dressed. If he was leaving, she was going too.

She came out of her room and saw her parents buckling on their chaps. She turned around and grabbed her new set of the leather protective covering for her legs, and the hair wrap. She looked in the mirror and grinned. This was the biker chick she would have been if the past years hadn't gone like they had.

She stepped back into the kitchen as her father was stomping on his shit kickers. Her mother was wearing a shoulder rig under her leather jacket, their colors were old school, but both of them carried the old-fashioned denim vests in their hands. The blade her father had earlier was nowhere in sight, but she would bet that it was somewhere on his person.

Rolf stood in front of her. She knew he was assessing her and wondered if she would be up for whatever happened tonight. She nodded her head, reached around him and took the colt from the counter to holster it in the small of her back.

"I'm a James, we don't run and we don't quit. I don't know who you plan to deal with, I don't care, I've got your back, Daddy, let's do this."

His grim smile grew rueful and he looked at June Bug, getting the nod from her. "The man that betrayed us and told Harry to leave and not come back is none other than the VP of the club. I plan to take care of the rat, and anyone who follows him. If the prez and the brothers decide to take sides, it is gonna get bad, so if I tell you to get lost, I mean it. Don't fuck with me on this one, baby girl. A pitcher of beer ain't gonna stop this from happening. He engineered the whole fuckin' thing, and ran our kids off so he could get in my former position. Bernell fuck face Cornell is getting what's coming to him tonight. I hate to think Trencher is in on this shit, but right now, hell I'm expecting anything to happen."

Harry kept updating the notepad and all the time she hadn't known he'd been so close. Why did he hide from her of all people, and where was he hiding out? Oh she planned to punch him in the gut when she saw him. To make her go through all that grief and pain was just mean. What in the hell was he thinking? She packed up the laptop and she was ready to go.

June Bug took the hard drive and put it in a bucket under the sink, before she walked out of the door.

Stevie hopped on the bagger with her father and June Bug started the Glide. Rolf leaned over and gave his wife a lip lock and Stevie thought of John. She looked away rather than flooding her mind with thoughts of his kisses. He'd probably forgotten her by now. She still felt bad about duping Lonnie, but one day, maybe he'd understand.

They had a short drive, but the most direct route was through the small town, and now Rolf knew why the two cops in the town had pulled him over last week. Bernell. That fucker, was not just a fuckin' stool pigeon, he was a goddamned traitor. They took the eastern route out of the area and went the long way around town.

The ride helped Rolf clear his head, made things separate from the red haze that threatened to take over. The times that happened were few, but he knew he was deadly when that happened. Those punks back at the bar yesterday were right about the berserker coming out, his heritage was Scandinavian, and his lineage could be traced back to the Vikings. His temper was legendary, and while he wasn't particularly proud of his exploits, he'd almost always been honorable. Knowing his former friend was behind all of the hurt that had befallen his family, he didn't know how he could filter the information into a non-violent solution, he actually didn't want to try.

The parking lot was still full of bikes, and Rolf pulled the bagger right up snug behind that fuck Bernell's ride. He waved his girls into the spot next to the fucker's scoot, and waited for them to dismount. "You all ready for the shit to splatter the walls?" He held his colors in his fist and June Bug pulled hers from the seat of her bike.

"I'm ready, Daddy, let's go sort this shit out."

Stevie had to smile at them, "Yeah, Daddy, let's do this."

Rolf walked in the door first, looked around and turned back to nod at his women. All three James family members walked slightly spread, Stevie cut over to the bar where the big screen was hung on the wall behind the long planks polished over the years with seat and beer. She walked around the bar, checked out the gaming system cords, and made her selection. She plugged the laptop in and began the feed to the big screen. She gave the bartender a look, and he held his hands aloft and backed away. She nodded her head. The brother grinned at the scene behind her back. She turned in time to see her mother throw her colors in the president's direction, and her father sneered at the big man as he shoved his vest under his nose, and left it on the table in front of him.

"I was born into this club, my fuckin' granddad started the fucker after the war because he and his war buddies wanted to keep in touch. They had each other's backs in the goddamned foxhole fighting the reign of that pencil lipped little cocksucker. They wanted to protect each other from their own fuckin' unjust laws and restrictions. My goddamned father bought it two weeks after he got back from that jungle in Nam.

"I've put my time in defending this country, and I took the shit that came down that had nothing to do with what I was doin'. I took all that, for the group. My whole family suffered for this group. I got the proof, and the reason. I'm done giving to this bunch of turncoat motherfuckers. There's no way that cocksucker did all this shit on his own, he ain't smart enough. I know in my gut he had backing."

Bernell started to rise, he was the VP after all, it was time this big motherfucker got what he deserved.

Rolf put his hand on the prez's shoulder. "You should know you are about to lose your Vice, so you might want to stay out of this, maybe you want to go to the bar over there and watch a movie while I take care of something. Your choice, I'm done talking either way."

He no longer cared what the others thought, he'd walked in the door and the red haze started falling, filling his brain. He walked over to where Bernell waited with a handful of men beside and behind him.

"Did you tell your pussy boys that it's a good day to die? Did you tell them that you're running drugs and causing families to be ripped apart?" The red rage grew brighter with every word he spoke, and Rolf reached for Bernell. The other man wasn't quick enough to escape his clenching fists.

Rolf hauled him forward and lifted him to his toes. "Did you really believe you would engineer my downfall and walk around like a lily assed prince? Motherfucker, you fucked the wrong family. Telling my boy not to come back was the dumbest fuckin' thing you could do, making the deal with Pascal was the second dumbest thing, stickin' around for me to find out you're still fuckin' with my kids. Well, you blue balled goat fucker, you gonna worry about it now."

He began shaking Bernell from the moment he had him in his grasp, the fucker was smirking at him, and that pulled the red veil down completely. Bernell went flying into the nearest table and Rolf was right behind him to grab him in his hands again. Everyone in the room could feel the bone crunch when the big man jerked his opponent over his raised knee into the ribs running alongside of the man's spine. If they didn't feel it in person, it made no difference, watching the VP's body arch and flopped helplessly in the legendary Rolf's hands gave them all the proof they needed.

Rolf yanked the arrogant bastard's arm up, jerking his bent body straight, while his fist planted itself dead center on Bernell's face. He shoved the two hundred pound man and laughed as Bernell landed face first into the wall. He slid down the wall and lay in the floor, not even a telltale twitch was seen, but Rolf threw three chairs at the possibly already dead man.

Two of Bernell's allies came at him, making the mistake of showing blades in their grasp. Rolf grinned at them and held out his hands in a come and get it gesture. He was busy with them and barely registered the sound of a gunshot behind him. The second shot didn't register as he enjoyed punishing his enemies. Hearing the pained screams of the man who he just crushed his wrist that had been holding a knife and Rolf used the hand holding the knife to shove it into his buddy's ribcage. Both men went down and stayed down, and when Rolf came after them to finish punishing them, they crawled away, leaving trails of blood and piss. He overturned tables and chairs to get them, roaring all the while.

He had no idea he was carrying a bullet in his lower back, and was bleeding, but June Bug had shot the fucking coward as soon as she saw which man held the gun still pointing toward Rolf. She then climbed up onto the bar with her Glock .40 pointing into the crowd.

Stevie told the bartender to move from the back of the bar to where she could see him and then joined her mother in policing the twelve men still standing or sitting in the room.

Trencher had taken Rolf's advice and skirted the fight to go over to the bar. He was lucky enough to have gotten a beer from Tim before the blonde beauty essentially shut the bar down by forcing Tim from his post. The video feed on the big screen was pissing him off, and now that he knew what had set Rolf off, he couldn't blame the man for wanting blood. In the first few frames, he'd recognized Rolf's boy, Harry, behind a classy bar setup, and he saw what good ol' Leon was doing right off. The tape must have been stopped there, and resumed with Stevie behind the bar, and Leon was there too. Seeing him sneak in the building at late hours of the night after Stevie disappeared from the video, opening the board of the small stage and packing bricks inside and tapping the wood back into place.

Twice he saw Bernell and Pascal join Leon in digging the packages from under the stage and hauling them from the building. The last few minutes of the video showed the vindictive grin on Leon's face as he set the fire.

This certainly explained a lot of what he'd been seeing in the past couple of years. He shook his head at his own stupidity, no wonder the brother was ready to do damage, Trencher himself was ready to hurt someone, but Rolf had earned his revenge, and as the president of Thor's Legion, he made the decision to ignore anything he didn't see tonight.

Standing close enough to kick him in the head was Rolf's woman. She was magnificent standing over the room with that 1911 in her hands, steady as a rock. He kept his head staring at the TV screen for the most part, but couldn't resist bending forward enough to see Stevie Lee James with a fuckin Glock, with the same stance as Momma, and he was impressed by the two women's bravery. He wouldn't have kicked either woman from his bed. June Bug was a rare bitch, there was no flirting with the men in the club on any level. She only had Rolf in her sights while they were in the clubhouse and he envied the closeness the two shared.

His own ol' lady was dead, and good riddance to her. She had been a faithless whore and he'd lost all feeling for her the day she aborted his kid. She'd been with that scum from the Swamp Rats, Pappy

D, and was rolled out of the door of a rusty fuckin' pick-up truck at the driveway. She was hopped up on some drug and started running down the road following the pick-up. The stupid woman had run right in the path of an eighteen wheeler. Curtis had been around then, he had dealt with the whole thing because Trencher had been drunk at the time.

He wanted to turn around and enjoy watching Rolf clean the clubhouse's rats out, but when it came for Church tomorrow, he wasn't going to say one fuckin' word against the man or his family. He was here, but hadn't seen a thing. Dammit.

*****

John watched the Swamp Rat leave the property and he nodded at the Prospect at the gate, and turned to go back inside the building. He barely cleared the doorway when he heard bikes pulling in outside. He kept going to the back room where he saw Baron walking into behind Gunner's wheelchair.

Myrtle had Melvin sitting his happy furry ass right up on the bar watching the people in the room. Myrtle handed him a beer as he walked past.

He needed to touch base with the two men before he headed out to find his woman.

Gunner was bitching about his confinement in the motorized chair, but he was grinning and optimistic about getting out of the damn thing in the next few weeks.

"Stretch is giving me too much sass, enjoying the fact she can outrun me, as soon as I am mobile her little ass will be feeling my wrath."

Baron laughed out loud, last night their woman had gotten a taste of the spanking she'd been courting, but touching her bare ass had led to other things and she'd sidetracked them with her passions. "Face it, bro, she has our number, and we wouldn't want her any other way."

He was still grinning as John walked in the door. "So we can safely say that you've been successful with your hunt?"

John nodded, "Taken care of, disposed of, now I have to go hunt down my woman. I got a text saying she had to take care of her problems because she wasn't the helpless woman she thinks I believe she is." He shook his head. She had no idea how he really thought about her, *soon*, he promised himself.

"I need some background on her and Viking. Do you know, I don't think she even knows Harry's road name? He spent a lot of energy keeping her in the dark about the club here. She thought that we would be mad at her for whining about the extortion shit. That fucker, Leon, wasn't with Candle when I caught up with him, so she's going to still be a target. Lonnie is still butt hurt that she gave him the slip, and the whole goddamned thing is a clusterfuck.

"When I get my hands on Viking, I'll be having a chat with the boy. I understand why he left, hell if it had been me, I would have done the same fuckin' thing. He neglected to make arrangements for her safety or let her know that he's alive, and that doesn't set right with me. He should have known she'd be vulnerable."

Gunner was shaking his head before John was finished talking. "Hang on a minute, man, the club let her down, he asked for us to keep an eye on her while he was gone. He was only supposed to be dead for a few months, but from the last text I got, he was following some dirty Fed fucker, then got himself fucked up when his scoot collided with a damned gator that ran out in front of him.

"He was following the fucker who was transporting the shipment at the time, so his stay in Florida was extended by over a month, and by then he had to catch the fucker on another run. He's been with his old club, Thor's Legion, in a charter down by Tampa. The last I heard, he was still working with Curtis. When I heard about Stevie being attacked, I sent him a text and the particulars."

John considered what he had been told. He knew that Viking had been with another club when he walked in the door, but he hadn't bothered to ask which club. The young brother had quite a resume if he had been with those guys. John had never been involved with any of the members of the outlaw bikers, but he'd heard plenty of stories.

It stood to reason, if Stevie's brother was a former Thor's Legion member, then she must be involved too. Fuck, he was resigned to the two day trip and he wasn't actually positive that she was with them. Sighing, he looked at Gunner.

"I don't believe she knew he was alive yesterday, so I don't think she would be in Florida with him. Where do you think would be the most likely place to begin? I could just get on the scoot and drive, but I'd like some idea of a destination."

Baron and Gunner exchanged nods and Baron told him about the tall skinny kid who walked into the club one night and asked to speak with him.

"The kid was good, he earned his rockers, and was loyal to the club. He brought his sister in the next day, and maybe a half a dozen times since then, but he said that she wasn't cut out for the life. The night you helped us torch that bike wasn't supposed to go down like it did."

"As for Thor's Legion, be careful, Stevie's ol'man is the biggest motherfucker I've ever seen. I've run into him a few times over the years, and he isn't the kind of man who will give anyone a pass when it comes to something he considers his or the club's. Last I heard was the parents were in prison, that's why Viking came here. He told me that he couldn't take his sister back either.

"He was nervous, but someone had put some balls on the kid, he didn't blink when Skids gave him shit, or any of the other's for that matter."

John was beginning to look impatient, and Baron gave him the information he'd came to them for. "If I was a betting man, I think it's a safe bet she went back to the club in 'Bama, that's the only place I would think to look."

John was halfway out of his chair when Gunner started to laugh.

"Man, you want to think about meeting the woman's parents, especially if Rolf is her father. That is one fucker I think could wipe the floor with your arrogant ass. I wish you luck, man, but I'll expect to hear you have to be carried from the man's tender taps on your head."

He was still grinning as John left the room after getting the address from Baron, and flipped him the bird. "Our boy has his work cut out for him."

CHAPTER THIRTEEN

John took the bagger back to the garage and exchanged it for his personal scoot. The ride wouldn't be as comfortable, but he liked it better and Stevie would want to drive her Jeep home, once he convinced her that she wanted to come back with him. That was going to be the hard part. The warnings about her ol' man didn't faze him, but then nothing much scared him anymore. He didn't plan to fight with the man, he'd try reasoning with him first.

He spent the night under the stars in his bedroll, once he'd found a grove of peach trees that had been picked clean. Looking into the night sky reminded him of the long nights in the desert and again during the time he began wandering in an attempt to find a place to call his own. Juanita had been his choice, his business was doing well. He'd been dragging ass about the family he wanted to have, and it was high time he did some catching up. He would be thirty-one in May, and the thought of little people running through the woods by his cabin made him smile.

He wasn't in love with Stevie, but he wasn't far from it. This nagging sense of loss was riding him hard since he read her last text. He had to admit that she caught his eye the first time he saw her coming into the garage, with her shiny gunmetal grey Jeep after her brother had given it to her for graduating college.

That day he'd thought she was younger than she actually was by a couple of years. She had a young looking boy with her that day, and every thirty-two hundred miles after she showed up by herself. She always insisted John do the oil change, her brother told her to take it to John to have it serviced, and she was stubborn about it. This last year, she'd stopped insisting he take care of the Jeep, she didn't have the time he usually made her wait for him to finish what he was working on to deal with the simple maintenance. He felt resentment for her defection, even if she had good reason for it.

He missed catching her staring at his ass through the glass partition separating the client waiting room and the shop itself. Twice he'd busted his knuckles while staring at her instead of paying attention to what he was working on. "Face it, dumbass, she's got your dick twisted up in a knot."

Sex with other women was physically satisfying, and now that he thought about it, every one of the handful of sex partners had been blonde for almost a year. *Fuck.*

He fell asleep with a swollen cock, and woke up to the sound of something moving nearby. The colt was in his hand within seconds and pointed toward the sounds of movement in the grass. It was a deer running through the trees being chased by a small pack of mangy dogs. None of the animals paid him any attention, and he thought about shooting the damn dogs, but he didn't want to draw attention to his resting spot, and hell, the laws of nature. The dogs were at least working for their dinner, he hoped the deer got away, but if he didn't, at least the meat would keep the dogs from attacking someone's kid or a farmer's livestock.

He groaned as he got up and stretched the kinks out of his back. Damn, it seemed the ground got harder each year. He took a piss and pulled a bottle of water from his saddlebags and rinsed his mouth, before drinking the clear liquid to quench his thirst. First stop would be for food and gas, it would be another long ride today to reach Wescott, Alabama.

He pulled into the parking lot of the former corset factory turned into the Mother Chapter for Thor's Legion. There were several scoots already there, and once he parked his bike, he admired a beautifully restored 45 flathead 1948 model. Painted a bright candy apple red, with added chrome accents, and he envied the owner.

He could hear muffled sounds that sounded suspiciously like a bar fight. The man sailing through the door confirmed his suspicions. Unfortunately for the man, whose neck got slammed by the heavy steel door, a long arm grabbed the head of greasy hair and tried to pull it back into the building without moving the door from where his neck was wedged between the door and frame.

John decided to save the cleaners the trouble of cleaning up a decapitated head and pulled back on the door handle to allow the unmoving body to be moved on the next jerk of the head. The noises of breaking furniture and the continuous roar of a deep voice gave him reason to sneak a look around the opened door and step inside.

He looked around to see several hands exchanging money while a man roughly resembling a Kodiak bear was tossing men around like they

155

were matchsticks. His hair was as wild as his eyes, and John had seen men in this condition before and wanted no part of what this man was dishing out.

He was tossing tables and chairs out of his way in his quest to capture the men that scrambled on hands and knees to avoid whatever punishment he was planning for them. One man was holding his bleeding side and had been heading toward the door when it was open. The crestfallen look on his face as the door slammed shut was almost comical, and the man hung his head in defeat. The berserker sent his huge booted foot under the bleeding man's ribcage sending the man onto his back, only to be picked up from the floor by his cut, and having a meaty fist pulverize his face and head.

John kept his eyes on the battle blinded man and backed himself up slowly to the bar. He backed into a barstool and quickly looked to see if he'd violated anyone's personal space. He was here for information, nothing more—and hopefully nothing less. The man sitting on the stool next to the one he'd bumped into was giving him an unfriendly look. His cut had a president patch and John nodded to him and introduced himself.

"I'm only here to ask where I can find a man by the tag of Rolf, I'm not here to cause any problems or interfere. Baron would have called, but there's not exactly a directory of phone numbers for MC clubs, I can give you his cell and you can get confirmation from him if you want."

Trencher eyed the motherfucker who had the balls to waltz into their clubhouse like he owned the fucker. "What business do you happen to have with

Rolf?" He ignored the sound of glass shattering behind him.

John looked at the men congregated near the wall, then looked at Trencher. "My woman is his daughter, I think she's here, or headed this way. Time to take her home."

Trencher looked ready to burst out laughing and shook his head. "Are you familiar with the James family?"

John shrugged his shoulders. "I know Stevie and Viking, Stevie calls him Harry. I've heard stories about the old man but I've never met him. I'm just here to collect my woman."

That statement caused Trencher to laugh, and it took a few minutes for him to calm enough to talk. "Do you see that big son-of-a-bitch that's probably finished with his fit about now?" He waited for the nod from John and jerked his thumb over his shoulder. "That is Rolf, and the lady standing right here next to me, the one with the gun in her hand? That's June Bug and Stevie is on the other end of the bar. The women of that family are as wild as the men."

He started laughing again as John's mouth hung open for a minute. His lips shut and his eyes narrowed.

He hadn't bothered to look at the women standing on the bar when he'd come in. He'd registered that someone was standing there but seeing the gun in the older woman's hand trained toward the men standing on the edges of the room made him look around to see Stevie standing five feet from her mother in an identical stance and with gun in her hand.

This wasn't his Stevie, this was a glorious Amazon biker chic princess. Seeing the way her vest cradled her tits made his cock stir in interest. The low riding jeans showed her pierced navel. She wore the same dangly sapphire blue jewel that hung from its curved ring. His lips had been there just a few days ago. The creamy skin that showed under the vest and above the waistband was maybe two inches, and he loved seeing it for himself, but he looked around to see who else was looking at his woman.

A skinny Prospect and two older men were watching her watch them and they were grabbing their crotches and gesturing for her to come on down off the bar and play with them.

He was torn between beating some gawking fuckers' heads in and dragging her happy ass down from her perch himself. He stepped around broken chairs and a body that was lying in his direct route to the woman he considered his own.

He stood directly in front of her and she finally looked down at him.

Stevie had been nervous standing there, but she would rot in hell before she let her parents down by not standing against the family's enemies. Her father was still prowling, looking for his adversaries and when she looked down, John was there. He was so handsome, so sexy wearing his leathers, the way the chaps cradled his crotch made her stare at that small space remembering what was hidden from her view behind the denim and leather. His hands were on his hips, and the look on his face was a mix of pissed John and turned on John. She wondered what he was mad about, and the big question was what was he doing here?

She lowered the gun in her hand and he reached out to pull her hand down to take the weapon, and he was so focused on her face and body language that he barely registered the roar behind him.

Too late, he saw Stevie's mouth open to say something to the man who grabbed him from behind and slammed his head into the wooden bar. John knew what was happening, but his eyes closed and his body crumpled to the floor.

Stevie screamed at her father to stop, but he was still in his haze of battle and she didn't know what to do, he was reaching for John again, and she set her gun down on the bar and jumped on the big man's back. She set her long arms around his neck and wrapped her legs around his waist, and held on for dear life. Her face was tucked into his neck as she screamed at her father to stop.

"Daddy, stop, he is a friend, he wasn't trying to hurt me, Daddy, please stop, you'll hurt him. Daddy, please, I think I love him." She was crying and was wetting his neck with her tears, but she didn't care about looking weak or vulnerable. She was happy to see John, her heart felt like smiling every time she'd laid eyes on him since the day they met, but if her father broke him into pieces, he wouldn't be the same thick-headed Neanderthal she cared about.

Rolf's hands held leather and cotton material. The soft hand that laid against his cheek didn't move from the spot it first touched. He was slowly registering something wet on his neck and the noise of a woman crying, begging her dad to stop hurting the man she loved? He shook his head trying to clear the red fog that clouded his brain. Another woman's voice was telling him how brave he was and how proud she was to have him as her man.

"Come back to me, Daddy, you destroyed our enemies, it's over now, let's go home, baby. Momma's tired and you need to help Stevie, she's crying for you."

The man's body dropped to the floor and June Bug was enclosed in Rolf's thick embrace. The big man was vibrating as the crazy left his eyes. The men still standing upright in the club breathed a sigh of relief. They weren't stupid enough to move from their places yet though, this was not a new thing for Rolf, the man was a tank when riled.

Finally, June Bug pulled her lower body back enough for Stevie to lower her legs to the floor and let her arms relax their death grip on Rolf's neck. She went to her knees as soon as she gained her balance, and crouched next to John's swelling head.

Someone handed her a plastic bag filled with ice and she didn't bother to look up when she thanked the man. Her eyes were only for John. His face was swelling with the side of his head and she wondered if she should call an ambulance.

June Bug was still petting and talking her husband down and wouldn't be any help but Trencher, the President of the charter, crouched on the other side of John's prone body while she pressed the ice on his face and head.

"He told me he came to take his woman home, but he knew he would have to deal with your father. He didn't know that the big guy was your father until I told him. The dumb fucker only had his sights on you once he saw you and your mom standing on the bar like that. He walked right passed Rolf to get to you." He lifted one of John's eyelids and could see the man had a concussion, fuck.

"We need to get him medical help, and from the looks of your pant leg, he's not the only one. Are you bleeding, or is it Rolf's blood soaking your thigh?"

Stevie looked down at her thigh and saw the blood that he mentioned. She had to swallow back a scream, it had to be her father's blood, and she looked up to search out where her parents were standing.

Her mother already stood at her husband's back with his shirt wadded up into a pad that she was pressing over the wound. Her head was on his shoulder and she was whispering next to his ear.

"I, uh, I need to get them help." She took a deep breath to center her thoughts before turning her attention back to Trencher.

"Do you have some way to transport them, or should we call an ambulance."

He grinned at her and stood. The girl was a James alright, cool as hell in any situation. He'd like to see how she reacted after the danger was past, but he had enough to worry about taking care of damage control right here. He walked behind the bar and pulled a key from the box under the bar and brought it back to her.

He handed the key to her. "I'll help get them loaded up, can you deal with the clinic?"

Stevie nodded her head and gave him a tired smile. "Sure, I found them on the side of the road like this."

She got a half smile from Trencher and he signaled for a couple of beefy brothers to carry John to the van. She followed the awkward shuffling trio out of the front door, while June Bug led a still wild looking Rolf out behind them.

CHAPTER FOURTEEN

Stevie drove them to the hospital in the next town, and let her mother deal with her father, while she gave the admitting nurse what little information she had about John. She had to tell them that she was his fiancée so they would allow her to stay with him and gain information. His wallet yielded his license and insurance cards, and a grand in cash.

She said that he'd fallen off his bike when he hit a woodchuck hole in the ground and hit his head on a rock. It was the only excuse she could think of to explain his injuries.

Luckily her father was treated and released within two hours. Unluckily for her, he was clear-headed and wanted answers about her relationship to the man he'd come close to killing.

She told him almost everything, while her mother sat with a small smile on her lips. "He's not as smart as I thought he was though, Trencher told me that he walked right into the clubhouse and once he saw me, he walked right into the path of your sight. How dumb is that?" She burst into tears, and had her face buried in her hands, and didn't see the look her parents exchanged.

Rolf looked at his daughter and shook his head, yep she's got it bad for the man. The thought made him sad, his little girl was a grown woman now.

June Bug was smiling gently at Stevie's bent head and turned to him, meeting his frown with her smile.

If there was anything more certain than the sun coming up each morning, June had as much faith in her heart knowing that Rolf loved their children more than life itself. Stevie had turned into a beautiful young woman in their absence, but this developing love with the big tattooed biker gave her a reason to really smile. She leaned in close to Rolf and whispered the new hope she had into his ear. "Just think, if this works out for them, we'll get babies to play with. Wouldn't grandpa sound nice to hear from a little one's mouth?"

*****

John was in the hospital for four days and Stevie stayed with him, talking to him, because he was in a drug-induced sleep to keep his pain levels down enough for them to drain the liquid from his eyelid and fluid that had gathered under his scalp from where the bone of his skull had cracked. Whatever they'd been giving him didn't remove all of the pain he was feeling because he moaned in his sleep. There were times his hands raised to clutch his skull, and Stevie had to pull his hands down to keep him from hurting himself even more.

The nurse aid that came in each day to give him a bed bath was much too pretty for her peace of mind, and Stevie didn't know that the offender noted with amusement the scowl she gave the woman.

Her mother had brought her a change of clothes each morning and stood guard while Stevie showered in the patient bathroom.

June Bug admired the man lying in the hospital bed. He was handsome without being a pretty boy, and he was certainly built well. The tats were beautifully done, her only concern were the marks for the dead. There were five very small skulls on his right shoulder and two on the left. She would ask Rolf, but she hoped this John Handy was not a killer. "You better listen up, tough guy, if you hurt Stevie, this little stay in the hospital will seem like a vacation compared to the place I'll put you."

On the third morning, they stopped giving him the pain meds and he began waking up slowly, as the medication wore off. He had to shield his eyes from the afternoon sunlight pouring into the room, because the light made the throbbing inside of his head become worse.

Stevie saw his reaction and rushed to pull the curtains around his bed to block the light.

She took his hand in hers and squeezed his fingers with her own. "Hey, big guy, I'm glad to see you're awake." She reached over for the Styrofoam cup of water and held the straw to his lips. "I think you're probably thirsty, and I'll ring for the nurse to let them know you are awake."

He was released on day four, feeling as weak as the day he'd been evac't from the Middle East with an almost identical skull fracture on the opposite side of his head, and three busted up ribs. The nurses back then weren't nearly as pretty as the ones here, and there had been no Stevie to hover over him at the time either.

Rolf was waiting at the house when June bug and Stevie took him home with them and he was grateful for the man's strength, even if he was the reason John was in this situation to begin with.

After being almost carried into the house by the big man, all John wanted to do was lay his head down and quiet the throbbing to a more acceptable level, but Stevie insisted on him being put into comfortable sweat pants and Rolf assisted her with that too.

After tucking the sheets around him and leaning over him to give his lips a quick peck, Stevie felt tears begin to flood her eyes, and she almost ran from the room. She walked past her parents where they sat at the kitchen table and kept going until she was in the carport where John's chopper sat. Sitting on the seat, she cried until she felt a man gathering her into his strong arms.

Rolf couldn't stand hearing his girl crying like this, he knew that she needed to let off the stress, but this was tearing him a new asshole for being such an enraged beast. Fuck this, there was only one thing he knew that would blow the sadness away, even for the short time they would be gone.

"Come on, Stevie, let's mount up, time for a blow-it-off ride." He reached over for June Bug's helmet and plopped it over his daughter's head and picked her up, only to set her on the bagger. He awkwardly hiked his long leg over the seat and started the bike. "I think we both need this, nothing like wind therapy to get your head straight."

June Bug heard the powerful growl of the scoot start up and leave, she saw that Rolf had taken Stevie for a ride and had to smile. It was almost like old times when the two of them would disappear for hours at a time when one or the other was in a snit over just about any reason, half of which she knew was manufactured just for the excuse to ride.

She took chicken from the freezer for dinner, checked her phone for messages, and went in to check on their houseguest.

John was sitting on the side of the bed gripping the mattress, and she didn't want to startle him but she knew he would fall down if he tried to stand too quickly.

"I'll be happy to help you to the bathroom if that's where you plan to go, but I can't pick your big ass up from the floor. So if you plan on being stubborn about it, you'll be on the floor for an hour or two. Rolf and Stevie are taking a ride, and you're the lucky man that has me as his only option."

John couldn't believe his bad luck, ever since he'd laid eyes on this family, his luck had been for shit. First his own stupidity for turning his back on Rolf in full battle mode, and now being forced to lean on a woman to use the damn toilet. Not just any woman, oh hell no, this one had to be Stevie's mother. He looked up at her standing next to where he sat and nodded, resigned to receiving help from the pretty woman.

June Bug laughed before bending down to give him her braced arm to help him balance. "You men aren't much different, you have no idea of how many times Rolf has been in your position. He's been shot too damn many times, one time he was smashed between a big rig and a minivan." She stayed with him until he could grab the sink to leverage himself up and down on the stool, and left him to his privacy for the next ten minutes while she straightened the bed sheets.

She heard the water running in the sink and waited close enough to the door for him not to feel crowded, but close enough to steady him.

She just held out her arm for him to place his hand on for balance as they made their way back to the bed.

"So, tell me about John Handy, I got your stats from your ID, and Rolf called Baron from your cellphone. He said you are one of the good guys, and let me tell you that went a long way toward setting out minds at ease about you and Stevie."

John didn't want to talk to the woman about himself, but if he hoped to leave with Stevie, he really had no choice. Telling her to mind her own damn business wasn't going to cut it with this family. His head was beginning to pound but it wasn't because of his injury.

"I want to thank you for the hospitality." He pushed himself up in a sitting position while she pulled the pillows up behind him for his back to rest against. He tried a smile and she smiled back. Maybe this wouldn't be so bad. *Yeah right.*

"Anything in particular you want to know? Let's see, I am thirty, a Taurus, my family is not close, and I own a garage in Juanita, Missouri. I've been a member of the Breed for almost three years now, before that I was a State Trooper out East, and before that I was a Ranger in the U.S. Army." He kept eye contact with June Bug while he spoke, and could read the appreciation for his candor in her expression.

168

"I met Stevie a while ago, and was impressed with Viking's little sister, but didn't make a move on her for obvious reasons. She's close to seven years younger than me and she was off limits to the brothers from the club. When Viking did his disappearing act, she was allowed to take over the bar, and she did a better job than he did."

He shifted his ass to change positions and hoped she would ask a question or something. She was giving him that "go on" look and it made him uncomfortable. For once he was happy his mom was such a distant, cold woman. If anything was in the way or had no purpose in her life, she tossed it. Knickknacks made by her kids for Christmas or Easter was included in that list of unnecessary things she tossed out after a day or two.

"We've been attracted to one another almost since we met, she gave me those small smiles and I couldn't resist, I talked to your son, and was told to leave her the hell alone, he wanted her to have a better life than a biker's ol' lady would be. He was right, I didn't know what might develop between us and couldn't make any promises of undying love and devotion, hell, exchanging flirty looks and smiles don't mean shit.

"A couple of weeks ago, I did a favor for the brother that normally picks up the payment and she told me about being targeted for extortion by those scum sucking fuckers, the Swamp Kings."

He heard a slight noise at the doorway to the room and saw Stevie and Rolf standing there and knew they must have been there for a while. Fuck. Stevie looked pissed and her father just looked thoughtful. There was a touch on his hand and a slight nod from June Bug with a small smile. Fuck it, they wanted full disclosure, they would get it.

"She showed me the bruises that a filthy son-of-a-bitch put on her when he broke into her home and killed her cat and raped her." He looked directly at Stevie, and she was staring at him when he said with more feeling than he knew. "That was the minute I didn't give a shit what her brother wanted, if he hadn't left her alone and vulnerable like that, she wouldn't have been hurt to begin with.

"She's mine now, and she will never want for anything I can provide for her. He doesn't want her around the club, fine, she can stay away from the clubhouse. The choice will be hers, not his, he lost his privilege of dictating her future actions when he chose to pretend to be dead and not telling her about it."

John shifted his gaze to Rolf, "She won't need to worry about that fucker coming back to hurt her again regardless of what she decides to do about us. He's no longer a threat to anyone."

He got a nod of acknowledgement from the older man and he watched as the giant left the room, leaving Stevie standing in the doorway.

June Bug patted his hand and leaned closer to him to place a kiss on his uninjured cheek. "Get some rest for now."

Stevie hugged her mother when she got close to the door, and June Bug didn't even try to draw her daughter's attention from the man on the bed.

John watched Stevie walk slowly toward him, and she stood over his bedside with her hands balled into fists at her waist. He could see that she was so pissed she was actively trembling in her rage, and he wondered what her damage was.

"My brother told you to leave me alone and you let him keep us apart? Being one of the brothers was more important to you than seeing if we could have made a good pair? I sat in that damned bar night after night hoping you would come in and ask me out, ask me for a cup of coffee, ask me the time of *fucking day*. I spent days wondering what was wrong with me that you wouldn't step up and ask me to go out with you. And all of this time, all of this *fucking time*, you've been using some stupid biker bullshit code to keep us apart."

She stomped her foot and when that didn't make her feel better, she doubled up her fist and slammed it into his stomach. She stared down at him while he was rubbing the spot where she'd hit him, and actually growled at him, turned around and slammed out of the room.

The look on her face made him smile, maybe now that she knew just about everything she would forgive him for keeping his word to her brother.

He sank down in the bed and fell asleep with a small glimmer of hope on his mind.

CHAPTER FIFTEEN

After two days of being confined to the room and his bed, John was thoroughly sick of the nurse/patient treatment from Stevie. She seemed to take particular pleasure in wearing shirts that showed her tits off, especially in the mornings when his cock was full-on-ready to fuck her sassy little ass.

She would bend down to straighten his blankets and brush her breasts on his arm or like this morning, she'd just bent from his waist to reach the foot end of the bed, and her tit had brushed down the length of his semi erect cock, bringing it to full attention. She acted like nothing happened but when she straightened up, he saw the tiny smile on her lips and the devious look in her eyes.

He snagged her wrist when she turned to go and pulled her down onto the bed, with her upper torso landing across his chest. He ignored her gasp of surprise, mainly because of the look of triumph in her expressive eyes before she narrowed them at him.

"Let me go." She tried to lever herself up on her arm, but John had her and wasn't letting her go. It was about time to her way of thinking, but she needed some payback for the way he'd wasted so much time when they could have been together already for almost three damned years. "Let me up, John, my parents will be back soon, they only went to the store, and if they find us in bed together you won't stand a chance of going back to the way things were before all of this happened.'

He shook his head no. "Stevie, you don't understand it, I realize that now, but men live by rules, we call them codes. You don't fuck with a man's bike, his club or his family, and you do not fuck a brother's sister. Especially one that is so much younger than I am." He could see that she wasn't buying the truth, but he was finished protecting Viking, fuck him. Right now she was more important than a long ago made promise to a man who left her vulnerable.

"Your brother was only slated to be dead for a few months when this whole damn thing started. He had setbacks and got sidelined for a few months, so he had to start over chasing down the drugs dumping grounds. That short fucker in the video is the same son-of-a-bitch who put your parents in prison, his brother was the foster father that was in the home they sent you to, and he planned to kill your brother. He's still out there somewhere, and Leon is still hiding under his rock.

"I took care of the fucker who hurt you, and I enjoyed every minute of making sure he wouldn't get up to hurt you or anyone else ever again. I got home, wanting to hold you and let you know you didn't have to fear the man any longer, and you were gone. You didn't trust me enough to deal with your problems and that fuckin' hurt to know my woman didn't trust me enough to stick around and talk about it."

"Now, I've tiptoed around your brother and your parents long enough, I want my woman."

He easily flipped them over so his leg pinned hers to the mattress, while his lips devoured hers. His hands began pulling her shirt up so he could savor her unbound tits. "So fucking beautiful, I love these beauties." He looked into her eyes. "And from the way your nipples are poking up at me, I'd say they like it. Hmmm, Stevie, take off your clothes for me so I don't rip them off you. I want my woman raw and wild, I want to see you riding my cock like you did the first morning we woke up together."

She felt shy when he mentioned that morning, but she wanted him, had wanted him for it seemed like forever. "My parents could come in any minute, John, we can wait until…."

The tug of the material covering her shoulders where he'd bunched the cloth was the only warning that he'd gotten tired of waiting for her to strip, and began ripping the thin cotton. His smile was predatory and she frowned at him, but he ignored that and yanked his own t-shirt over his head, tossing it behind himself and bent down to lick and suck her nipples.

She arched her back to push her breasts harder into his hands and mouth, and loved hearing him moan. He was noisy as he licked his way over her skin, but it turned her on to know that he loved giving them both such pleasure.

Her hands went to the waistband of her jeans and found one of his hands already there working on the button and zipper of the denim. The discovery made her giggle and she raised her hands to hold his head to her breast.

"I hope you don't plan to tear my jeans off, I only brought two pairs with me and I might need them." She got a bite on the nipple for her teasing, and gasped. "Oh, John, God that feels so good."

He let the tight nipple leave his suctioning mouth and sat back against the headboard. "Take them off, I wouldn't want you to leave this room totally naked, but right now I am not in the mood to wrestle with clothing." His hands reached for the tight buds again as she backed off the bed and slid her tight jeans down her legs.

When she stood next to the bed naked and nervous looking, he had to smile. He held out his hand and she put hers into it. He had half expected her to run from the room, but she stood her ground and he was thankful for the trust she was giving him.

He pulled her over his lap and kissed her beautiful lips, turning the kiss into an all out assault on soft wet tissues of her mouth and tongue. He broke the kiss and leaned forward to push her torso into lying face up between his spread thighs.

His hands roamed at will over her skin and she gasped when he added harder pressure than she'd ever felt to her nipples. "Oh I, that, is so, harder, do that again."

He smiled at her, loving her enthusiasm for the things he did to enhance her pleasure. His hands cupped the cheeks of her ass and raised her pussy up to his hungry mouth. His tongue licked at her clit and traced the hood covering the tiny muscle before sliding down to the entrance of her pussy. He loved the taste of her juice and lapped every trickle that escaped her vaginal entrance. Moaning as he shook his head fast while still sucking hard on her flesh seemed to amp up her enjoyment and in turn made his cock feel like it would explode. He tongue fucked her hole and she came up into his mouth, his tongue was feeling the flutter and clamp of her pussy and he pushed it as deep as he could reach. She was clutching her breasts and pinching her own nipples.

"Oh God, don't stop, don't ever stopppp… Oh fuck." Her back bowed and pushed her hips upward again. She was lost in pleasure. "What you're doing….don't stop, yes right there, yesss….." Her orgasm hit fast and caused her body to jerk in time to the tongue in her pussy's rhythm.

John saw her head snap back, then felt her thighs tighten around his shoulders and doubled the strokes of his tongue for her to reach the pleasure that waited for her. When it hit her, he continued to stroke his tongue over her soaked flesh, making encouraging noises that vibrated through his mouth to her sensitive clit, which was standing outside of its hidden covering. One last tap of his tongue, and she began to scream and grab at the bedding next to his hips.

"That's right, honey, it only gets better." He lowered her hips to his lap where his cock was immediately sliding between the soaked slit of her still clutching pussy lips. "Now that's a pretty sight, my cock is getting harder from just the sight of your lips sucking at the shaft of my cock."

She laughed lightly and levered herself to her elbows to see what he was staring at. "Oh wow, that does look hot." She gave a short pump of her hips and shivered from the delicious stab of pleasure from his cock bumping her still sensitive clit. "Hmm, I like that too."

He was done playing, his cock was ready to burst and he wanted to be inside of her when it did. He reached down to help her sit up, and then lifted her ass up enough for his cock to sink inside. "Hmmm, oh yeah, just like that. So fuckin' tight, your pussy is still greedy, isn't it, baby, I can feel her clenching each inch I give you. Fuck, woman, I'm dying here, move, ride me."

Stevie raised and lowered her hips onto his but couldn't maintain a rhythm in the position she was in. "I need some help here, big man, all I want to do is sink your cock deep inside of me and grind down on you until I come again."

She was doing just that and sank her nails into his shoulder blades as she sank her teeth into the tight muscle covering his chest, a growling moan hummed along his chest and went right to his cock. The cum came shooting from his balls even as his hands grabbed her hip and thigh to shove deeper until he was a deep as he could get. "Oh fuck, baby, come for me, I can feel you, so damn hot." His arms wrapped her tighter to his chest, and feeling her nails rake down his back finished him off, no way was he giving this woman a chance to take this away.

John licked her neck and whispered into her ear, "I licked you so you're mine now."

She burst into laughter and hugged him back, "I can't believe you would say something like that, but I like the idea."

By the time they were dressed and left the bedroom, her parents had returned and were busy putting groceries away. That was their story and Stevie didn't want to question why her father threw a box of noodles at them and told them to get lost when she and John started into the kitchen. They changed direction and went into the family room to wait for the older couple to finish doing their thing. Stevie kept blushing and shaking her head and John couldn't help but laugh.

"Be happy for them, they're still young and can enjoy a healthy sex life. It gives me hope for us in the future." He pulled her closer and looked into her beautiful eyes, his hand raised and brushed her hair back.

"Stevie, I know you think it was a mistake for me to respect your brother's wishes, and maybe it was, but a man has to live by some rules, and what's done is done. I want a future with you, and if that's what you want too, then we will deal with whatever comes our way. What do you think?"

What did she think? "We've wasted so much time already that I am sick and tired of waiting around for something to happen, I'm tired of taking my Jeep in for oil changes and mysterious noises, just to look at a man I couldn't get to ask me out, and was too proud to ask you myself. I thought that you liked me, but something was wrong with me." She poked him in the chest to emphasize her point.

"And, you need to understand something, I don't like it when you go all Neanderthal on me. Just because I am a woman doesn't mean I can't handle reality or the truth. So don't expect me to just let you hide important things from me because you're being an arrogant asshole. I'm a big girl and can deal with it." She took his cheeks between her hands and stretched up to kiss his lips, "We can deal with things together, it's called trust."

The rumbling shout from the kitchen had them looking at each other and grinning. Stevie felt John pulling her hand from his shoulder to hold in his big hand.

"All I can promise is I will do my best to share, but you have to open your mouth and tell me when I am shutting you out. Someday I will break down and tell you about my parents, but trust me, they are nothing as great as yours are. So what do you say? Are we going to do this? Live together, share our lives, whatever you want to call it?"

She really wanted to make him wait for her answer, but they'd wasted years already, *fuck that*, she made her decision, *both feet, Stevie, if you want this then do it*. She nodded.

"I want this, I want to have an us, does that make sense? I tried not to let you inside my heart, it hurt for you to act like I was just another woman hanging around, and once Harry was gone, I needed someone to lean on, but the only man I really wanted was ignoring me, so I tried dating other men."

The look on his face was gratifying, the scowl at the mention of her dating other men made her smile and shake her head.

"They weren't you. Not one of them was a big, stubborn assed Neanderthal, and none of them made me want to cuddle close and rest my head on his chest." She got another mouth fucking kiss for her confession.

Laughter from the next room put smiles back on their lips, and John sighed.

"Now I get to have a man to man with your father. If he busts my head again, I might need to rethink this relationship." He laughed when her fist made a solid connection with his stomach. "If he doesn't like the idea, I'll just kidnap your ass and take you to my lair in the woods."

She grinned wide, "I happen to love your lair, big guy, you won't have to do much kidnapping to get me there."

Dinner was fun with her parents, and she wasn't nervous at all when John invited Rolf for a run and a beer at his favorite watering hole. The men left, and she sat with her mother talking.

"Do you love him, baby?" Stevie nodded.

"It feels like I've loved him forever, and I am so pissed at Harry for taking my choice away, and keeping us from being together before now." She drummed her fingernails on the Formica topped kitchen table and shook her head to clear the anger from her brain.

"Harry refused to allow John to ask me out, in fact I have a suspicion that he probably warned all the club brothers to leave me alone. I think he wanted me to marry some suit and tie type of man and live in the suburbs away from MCs. Every time I wanted to go to the Breed's club, he made up excuses not to have me there, and now that I've figured out why, he isn't around for me to yell at him."

June Bug patted her hands, calming the drumming, "Baby, men are dumb as dirt sometimes, Harry was doing his best to protect you and you know it. I understand what you're saying, but trust me, when you have a daughter, and a son, the boy will still try to boss her around. It's just natural in this family. I'm happy that you have a good man who loves the socks off your feet." She smiled and let a light laugh escape her lips.

"Did I ever tell you what happened when my father found out that his little princess had gone and got herself knocked up by a biker punk?"

By the time she'd finished her tale of teenaged parenthood, both women were laughing at the men in their lives. "It's inevitable that your man got beat up a little."

They were still catching up when the men got back, and from the sound of their voices, they hadn't come back alone.

*****

The sight of her brother walking into the kitchen was followed by someone she vaguely remembered seeing before but couldn't place him. Harry looked like he'd been in a bad fight, his lips were bleeding and there was a cut over his rapidly blackening eye.

June Bug hopped up and stood by the chair, waiting for her son to come to her. He didn't hesitate to make a beeline to his mother, uncaring that everyone in the room was smiling to see the reunion between mother and son. June Bug was dangling in his arms, crushed in his tight embrace. She kept running her hand over his head, and scolding him for staying away for so long.

Stevie looked back toward the door and was surprised he was also wiping a small trickle of blood from his mouth. She glanced toward her father, and saw that he was watching the reunion of mother and son. He was smiling in approval, with no visible signs of being in a fight.

She knew then that John and Harry had gotten into an argument, and wondered what had happened, but her place was with her man. She got up and went to him, lifted her fingers to his swollen lip and wiped the last drop of his blood that had beaded on his skin.

"I don't suppose this had anything to do with me, did it?" She took his hand and urged him toward the bathroom so she could clean his face, and check for any other injuries. "I think we need to go home tomorrow, you keep getting hurt around here, and I expect you to be in perfect shape when I move into your lair. I have been making plans for that big tub and I also plan to ravish you in the woods."

Life was going to be good; she'd waited long enough to start it.

ABOUT THE AUTHOR

RYDER DANE

I write about MC Groups aka Biker Books, because I've lived with Motorcycles my entire life. It made me smile when a reviewing reader said that there was a realistic feel to my writing! Having been an "Old Lady" since I was 19 gives me the advantage of using a few real details of MC life. I am very happy to bring readers my stories and having them invest in my characters' lives.

Website: Ryderdane.com

Books by Ryder Dane
Big Dog (Burning Bastards MC Book 1)
Nomad's Fall (Burning Bastards MC Book 2)
Charlie's Heart (Burning Bastards MC Book 3)

Sanctuary Within the Breed
(Lucifer's Breed MC Book 1)
Integrity Has No Bounds
(Lucifer's Breed MC Book 2)
Starting Over (Lucifer's Breed MC Book 3)